THE INN
OF
WAKING
SHADOWS

THE INN
OF
WAKING
SHADOWS

KARLA BRADING

Gomer

First published in 2018 by Gomer Press,
Llandysul, Ceredigion SA44 4JL

ISBN 978 1 78562 272 4

A CIP record for this title is available from the British Library.

This book is published with the financial support of the
Welsh Books Council.

Printed and bound in Wales at
Gomer Press, Llandysul, Ceredigion
www.gomer.co.uk

For the Littlest Pidge,
you were the best thing that ever happened to me.

One

It was downright hard being the only person at school to grow up in a 900-year old house. Sorry. Not a house. A pub. Even worse: a pub that was supposed to be haunted. Why couldn't Emlyn have grown up at the centre of a busy terraced street, where the neighbours gathered to murmur about the lack of parking? Or bickered over Marge in number one, who still hadn't taken her decorations down from Christmas? When his classmates all traded similar-sounding stories about where they lived, he was always the weird kid who lived in the haunted pub.

If his parents wanted to be a little 'out there,' Emlyn thought a farm would have been acceptable, as long as they didn't expect him to milk any cows at the crack of dawn. Or collect eggs in a manky chicken coop. Or – perish the thought – shovel manure.

But when his mam and dad had finally moved them out of the Skirrid Inn and into a proper house next door, it wasn't to make Emlyn's life easier. No, it was all part of a new plan to expand their humble little public house into a wildly unnerving, historically haunted bed and breakfast. But change can be a scary thing. Would the freshly painted upper bedrooms and noisy wooden floors be satisfactory enough for the paying public? Would guests come and lay their weary heads on the goose feather pillows and buy the inn's home-cooked roast dinners when evening fell? Would the visitors whisper of the Skirrid's unsettling atmosphere and encourage others to spend a spooky night under its roof?

Did people even want to be frightened when the lights went out?

Emlyn watched his parents fret over the bookings day in and day out, but ever... so... slowly, curious tourists trickled in. Tourists who had come to marvel at the surrounding, stark-green, Welsh hills. Some of them were artists; others were poets or hikers. They all loved gobbling up a homely pub meal after a trek across the glorious Brecon Beacons. Tired from their adventures and inspired by the views, the guests were captivated by the stories of ghostly characters roaming the halls of Emlyn's old, creaky home.

Business was pleasant, manageable and (kind of) peaceful.

Then television got involved and everything changed again.

'Emlyn!' his Mam snipped at him from over the

bar. She was carefully unwrapping something from a mass of white tissue paper, the scrunching noise almost as irritating as a wasp pummelling a closed window (one of Emlyn's pet hates).

He had been sitting alone at a table in the dining area, immersed in a rather thick book, with just 40 pages left. Emlyn was determined to have it finished before the day was through. To him, there was nothing more satisfying than devouring the last sentence of a good story, and dwelling on it later as he drifted off to sleep.

But not today.

'Take this,' his mam said, approaching the table. She handed him a bell. It was petite and covered in delicate lilies, painted in watercolours of pinks and purples and lush greens. Emlyn took it between his thumb and forefinger; the motion producing a little tinkling sound. Emlyn stared at his mam questioningly.

'Err, thanks for this. I guess.' The tinkling ceased.

She rolled her eyes. 'It's for Room Three. Remember? I told you the other night, at dinner: we need to start thinking more about making a show of this place. Business is thriving now, Em. People want to be entertained! They want history! They want props!'

She wasn't exaggerating either. After a popular

ghost-hunting programme had featured the Skirrid Inn in an episode, exploring its renowned spiritual activity, guests had started pouring in from far and wide, eager to catch a glimpse of something unexplainable. Hungering for a glimpse of the spooky and surreal, they too wanted to be shaken by the house's unnatural inhabitants. The film crew had caught some particularly disturbing footage: picture frames pushed over by invisible forces, knocking sounds on walls and footsteps clonking over upstairs beams when all living hands and feet were clearly accounted for. A few of the crew even claimed to have felt hands around their neck, choking them.

Suddenly, the Skirrid Inn was one of the most exciting venues in the whole of Wales.

Emlyn, however, was a sceptic when it came to ghosts. An un-believer. For a boy who had lived in what was now Room One of the inn for the best part of his life, he had never experienced anything he couldn't justify with fact, or science, or rational thinking. He'd earnestly watched the television episode (after being warned by his parents on filming day to give the crew space). But as he'd watched the flying picture frames with a furrowed brow, he couldn't help but feel tricked by the alarming footage. After all: some of the best magicians could convince a thousand minds that they were levitating when they weren't. Emlyn was, quite frankly, not so easily swayed.

Yet, in light of that programme, his once-home became a hotspot for hunters.

Ghost hunters.

'Hello! The Skirrid Inn!' Emlyn's mam announced grandly as she picked up the trilling phone. There were noises of understanding from her lips and a: 'Let me check my book and see what nights we have available...'

Emlyn stood, closing his book. His mam pawed the heavy-duty diary with excited hands and shooed him away, adding a jab of her finger towards the ceiling and a second jab towards the bell.

Room Three, he thought, glancing at the lily-painted object lying in the palm of his hand. What on earth did it need a bell for? Was his mam going to allow guests to start ringing for their breakfasts? Surely not.

He located the key hanging from a clearly labelled hook in the kitchen and shuffled into the hallway to the heavily varnished staircase. The wood was old and authentic, dipping in the centre of each step from extensive wear. So many shoes had been up and down them. And it wasn't just the shoes of people who had paid to stay overnight. There were those who just came in to eat lunch, but would timidly request a tour – just a quick gander at the fabled rooms. Emlyn's parents never turned them away, instead cheerfully offering up the chance to admire every nook and cranny, reeling off historical facts as they went.

Thinking only of returning quickly to his book now, Emlyn made his way upstairs. The keys and the bell tinkled in unison with each footfall. He was so enraptured by thoughts of reading that he almost tripped and swallowed his own tongue when, from the corner of his eye, he spotted a figure looming above him –

A nondescript figure, cloaked in darkness –

And a hangman's noose tied around his neck.

Two

'HAAAAAAAH!' the figure howled. 'Your face!'

Emlyn assumed an expression of utmost disapproval as his dad slid the noose from over his head. It had been loose and untethered. A piece of thick rope that he'd fashioned into a prop.

'Why so ghostly pale, son?' he jested, wiggling the noose as if it were a snake curled dangerously in his arms.

'All right, Dad. Gerr off,' Emlyn moaned, swatting him away.

'Do you like it? Your mam wanted it on the old beam. Makes sense, really. If you've got the original beam from real criminal hangings, you might as well sling a noose on it for entertainment.'

Emlyn frowned. 'Isn't it a bit... unfair?'

'Unfair?' His dad's brow furrowed. 'How so?'

'Well... people died here. And you've got a rope to tie to a genuine piece of history, for guests to gawp at.'

'There's nothing unfair about making a living, boyo,' his dad said seriously. 'Business is –'

'– thriving,' Emlyn cut in. 'I know.'

'Right. Exactly. This place is becoming a museum. A historical landmark! A place to remember those who passed away here. If anything, the dead would appreciate the effort.'

'If you say so,' Emlyn said, ascending once more.

'Where are you going?'

Emlyn tinkled the bell dramatically.

'Ah! For our good maid. Excellent!'

'We're getting a maid?' Emlyn looked puzzled again.

'No, no! The maid. You know? The maid who died here? What's her name?' Emlyn's dad clicked his fingers, but couldn't summon the right word. 'I think I'm having a senior moment.' He shrugged it off. 'Anyway. Why employ a maid when we have you?'

'Har dee har har,' sang Emlyn as he started up the stairs again. His dad laughed as he leant over the banister, attaching the noose to the old beam. He positioned it exactly where the original noose had created grooves, worn deep into the wood from people thrown off the top level and left to swing as cruel punishment for their crimes.

Emlyn knew his mam would check all the props she'd become so heartily invested in, so throwing the bell onto the double bed in Room Three was not an option. He eyed up the windowsill, debated one of the bedside tables, then eventually settled on a cabinet full of empty, decorative perfume bottles that his mam had gathered over the years from charity shops.

Giving the bell one last tinkle, Emlyn set it down in the centre of a vacant doily.

'That would wind me up tight, listening to that thing ringing for me all day,' he murmured, locking the door behind him. Downstairs again, he returned to his book, and was soon happily distracted again from the nonsense he was forced to live around.

*　　*　　*

Bang.

The door rattled home on its hinges as she appeared.

The bang was deafening – sharp in her ears so used to silence.

Where had she been? She remembered floating in a realm of no light or dark – just thick, grey murkiness, and a cloying, sticky warmth that seemed to stick to her. Buoying her sickeningly in a colourless river. She'd had no clue how many days had passed there, only a vague knowledge that eternity was both behind and ahead of her.

Her thoughts had unravelled there like the hem of an old skirt.

Who she was had been lost to her.

Until now.

A young woman stood before an unfamiliar cabinet, staring at the small, patterned bell that rested on it. The bell wasn't familiar at all, but the sound –

Her name came to her lips suddenly and clearly, and her mind roared with returning memory.

Her heart, however, remained silent.

'Fanny,' she whispered with a snag in her throat. 'I'm Fanny Price. And this is where I died…'

* * *

'You're up late, aren't you?' asked a woman from a nearby table. She wore a baggy T-shirt of many colours and had big gold hoops in her ears that were so thick it was a wonder they didn't pull her ears off. A camcorder rested by her elbow.

'Tomorrow is the last day of the summer holidays,' Emlyn pointed out with a shrug. Why were people always so curious about him? Could they never leave him read in peace? Not to mention, eight o'clock wasn't what he deemed 'late'. 'Mam wanted me to stick around tonight and help with the washing up when everyone's finished eating.'

If he had had his own way this evening, he certainly wouldn't still be sitting among rowdy tourists. But his dad had finished the chores and slipped away to watch football, leaving Emlyn to help close up. It wasn't often, but the match was a 'big one' apparently. And waiting to watch the highlights wouldn't cut it.

'You live here? In this building?' The woman raised a bushy eyebrow and leaned forward.

'When I was little, I lived in here. Now we live next door because –'

'Have you seen anything?' the woman interrupted, her eyes flashing eagerly.

He had known this question was coming, of course. It was always the same with the ghost hunters.

They lapped up every dreg of information about the inn, thriving on the summarised scraps that guests had written in the log book about experiences during their stay. They listened intently to the locals at the bar who readily produced memories of pint glasses miraculously hopping onto the floor and shattering into tiny pieces.

'Um. There's been nothing I couldn't explain,' Emlyn said, abandoning the book with a pent-up sigh that he had to stifle with a quick yawn. 'I've heard some things. But –'

'What things?' She waved a hand frantically at a man who was returning from the toilet. He wore brown cord trousers that had a splash of Emlyn's mam's special lamb cawl on the knee – a dinner time slip-up.

'I don't know. Scratching, I guess? It was probably just a cat wandering down the lane. Or, it could even have been a cow or sheep, loose from one of the fields.' Emlyn was fluffing up his story a bit. He didn't 'guess' it was an animal. He knew darn right it had been. But he liked giving the punters something to think about.

'He lives here,' the woman explained wistfully to the man, who was stroking his thick moustache and eyeballing his half empty glass of wine. His amber eyes lifted.

'Well there's a thing, indeed,' he said. 'You must have been properly spooked by now, I take it?'

It was at this point – in these frequently recurring conversations – that Emlyn felt he shouldn't be honest about his lack of belief in ghosts and ghouls. Telling his parents' guests that they were talking nonsense wasn't good for business, after all.

'I can never be sure of anything I see,' he began, with an eerie tinge to his voice. 'Mam has seen glasses moving. Heard voices. Seen shadows. Dad too.'

'And yourself?' the woman pried.

'Nothing yet,' he said. 'I must be missing a sixth sense or something?'

'Does the Devil really drink from that tankard?' the moustached man queried, pointing to the shelf over the fireplace. A sturdy silver tankard stood proudly in place, full to the brim with mead. It was said that the Devil visited in the night for a quick pint before returning to his merry mischief elsewhere. 'Has anyone ever claimed to have seen our fabled, pointy-horned sinner?'

'There's been mention of a shadow leaving the fireside in the guest book comments a few times.' Emlyn gestured to the burgundy book on a small table laden with leaflets for other adventures that could be had in the area.

His inquisitive guests stared at the scratched silver tankard. They waited for a moment, breath held, to see if in those heartbeats they might catch a glimpse of forked tail and horns emerging.

'I've never seen him,' Emlyn confided. Though it probably went without saying.

The man and woman's chests lost their puff and they seemed to shrivel in their seats. Disappointed.

'We're going to be filming most of the night,' the woman explained. 'Maybe we'll get lucky? You can't have a place with 182 people hanged by the neck and not generate some creepy energy, eh?'

Emlyn offered a smile. 'Well, if you see anything, be sure to tell my mam or dad in the morning. They love feedback.'

The woman patted the camcorder. 'Oh, we will. The whole world will know about it.'

Emlyn didn't doubt that for a one second.

Three

As it was, the couple with their camcorder caught zero footage of spectral lights, or of unknown faces in the dark. They stayed in Room Two – the room that was said to be the old court, where people's wrongdoings were dissected and sentenced by the bullying Judge Jeffreys. But other than a few unprovoked creaks, nothing solid came of the evening.

For some unlucky guests, that's just how it was. Ghostly activity was never exactly a guarantee, no matter how much money they paid for the night.

'It gave me chills, though,' the lady shared at breakfast, as Emlyn sat on a table close by, eating his crumpets with lots of salted Welsh butter. He'd finally finished his book whilst tucked up in bed the previous evening and was already perusing the crisp pages of a new one. 'You can't doubt there's something strange about this inn,' the lady added.

'The hairs on my arms stood on end all night. Even though I was perfectly warm,' the man with the moustache agreed. He chewed as he talked, chunks of egg dancing between his teeth for all the world to see.

'Did you sleep at all?' Emlyn asked them. It always fascinated him, the lengths guests would go to see something. The common practice (Emlyn had witnessed) was to glug energy drinks or coffee to give them the zing they needed to make it through until morning. He'd tried, once, to stay up reading for a whole night – a kind of dare to himself, because his parents would not have approved if they'd known. But after numerous changes in position on his bed, rapid blinking and even a gentle slap to his cheeks, he'd fallen into oblivion by 3 a.m.

'I had an hour's kip,' the man chuckled. 'She had about three.'

The 'she' he so fondly referred to smiled and touched the top of the man's hand. 'The four-poster bed just sang to me as the night wore on. Silk sheets. Big pillows. Bliss!'

'We'd definitely come again,' the man said. He had a clear, unquenchable desire to feel the adrenaline rush of ghost hunting once more. 'This place isn't finished with us yet.'

Emlyn tried not to smirk at the bit of scrambled egg caught in the man's moustache. He returned to his book instead.

When his breakfast was finished with – leaving little more than a greasy butter stain on the plate –

he handed the cutlery and crockery to his dad in the kitchen, who always let his mam have a lie-in if she'd pulled off an evening shift. ('She needs her beauty sleep,' he'd wink).

'Shouldn't you be sharpening pencils ready for tomorrow?' his dad asked jovially, as he rinsed the plate in the sink. Tomato juice slid down the porcelain like blood.

'It's comprehensive school. The 'writing with pencil' days are dead!' Emlyn called over his shoulder, leaving the inn and its sleep-deprived guests to tackle a new day. His plan was to prep everything he needed for school and then relax (though not necessarily in that order). He'd maybe watch a few DVDs, and he was due a lengthy search of the internet for books he could ask his parents for. As he was too young to get a proper job yet, his mam and dad had agreed to buy Emlyn books of his choosing – keeping his shelves stocked and his imagination fiery – as long as he kept up with chores around the house and the Skirrid Inn. He was allowed a choice of two hardbacks a month, four paperbacks a month, or one hardback and two paperbacks a month. A pretty sweet deal for any book lover.

Emlyn took great pleasure in trawling through the net: reading reviews, judging book jackets (which he knew he wasn't really supposed to do), revisiting author webpages to check for new releases and generally making lists of the books he'd like to read in payment for mopping floors, dusting windows, washing dishes, or banging the rugs and curtains clean in the garden.

With a belly full of breakfast, he entered the house. His mam was lightly snoring in the room upstairs next to his own, with a lukewarm coffee beside her bed. Dad always left a fresh mug on the bedside table and she usually roused in enough time to drink half of it before it went stone cold.

Emlyn crept by and pounced onto his bed, careful not to crush the pages of the book in his hand beneath his gangly bulk. He was tall for his age, which his mam reminded him of regularly when shopping for trousers that were always too short in the leg ('Waist like a bean sprout and height like a climbing vine! You're like your dad,' she'd say). But with his great length, Emlyn thought he looked too 'stretched' – like the character he'd read about as a kid who was so flat and long that he could slip under doorways and be folded up into the shape of an envelope. Emlyn was long all over. His arms, he felt, resembled a sloth's. Even his hair was long – dark and floppy, falling messily over one eye.

He turned to his wide window, with its crisscrossed pattern on the glass – something his mam called 'quaint cottage décor'. To Emlyn, it looked like fancy prison bars.

From his vantage point, he watched the Skirrid Inn's guests lingering outside, taking last-minute photos beneath the hanging sign and pointing up at the old building. There would be a fresh lot of thrill-seekers arriving before he knew it, but his parents had fixed in place three nights of rest: Mondays, Tuesdays and Thursdays – unless, of course, Halloween fell on one of them. In that instance, they opened their doors to satisfy the ghost hunters that came searching for the ultimate Halloween scare.

'Emlyn?' came a call.

His body gave a jolt of surprise. He'd been wrapped up in observing the people below him, all talking and laughing and slowly dispersing back to their cars, their homes, their lives. Leaving the ghosts behind them. Returning to normality.

He could hear his mam stirring in her bed.

'Yeah?'

'Everything okay?'

'Yeaaaaah.'

'Did you notice any burnt toast on people's plates?'

The burnt toast ordeal was a permanent niggle in his mam's head. A guest had written a review on some travel website and had mentioned their experience at the inn was 'pleasant enough', but the toast at breakfast had been black on one side. His mam had had nightmares about it ever since and scolded his dad for such ghastly and unacceptable neglect in the kitchen.

'It all looked good to me,' Emlyn assured her.

'Thank God,' she sighed sleepily, before adding, 'Come in here with me for a bit.'

He closed his eyes and plonked the back of his head against the deep blue of his bedroom wall. He just wanted to stay in his room with his single-person squeaky bed, washed out grey bedsheets, posters of inspiring book quotes and neatly lined shoes in front of the radiator.

'Emlyn?'

'I'll be there now.'

His mam was upright with the mug pressed into her chest, held with both hands. She was wearing her pink and silver striped pyjamas, with the pocket at the front that she usually stored her reading glasses in. (They were currently on his dad's pillow.)

'Sit with me for five minutes.' She patted the duvet.

Emlyn perched on the edge, shimmying his backside left and right to get his balance.

'Ah, my boy,' his mam sighed, tenderly pushing

the dark strands of hair from his eyes so she could see his face better. 'Big school in the morning. I can't believe it.'

'Mam –' Emlyn groaned, swiping his fringe forward so that the choppy style flopped over forehead again. It was the most popular look you could currently go for and it had taken him ages to grow it long enough.

'Oh! You and that hair. You can barely see your handsome face. Don't you want girls to see your eyes under there?'

'Not really,' he replied.

She clucked her tongue. 'Just remember what we talked about. Any trouble: tell a teacher. Be extra polite: open doors for other students and staff. Don't be afraid to be the first to say 'hello'. Eat Polos instead of chewing gum if you feel the need; it's less mess. And smile, Emlyn. For the love of God! You're the only boy I know with a full set of teeth untainted with fillings and we barely see them.'

'That's because there's barely anyone worth showing.'

'Don't be silly. You need to start being positive.' She smiled affectionately and tapped him on the knee. 'You'll let me take a photo of you in your uniform before you go tomorrow?'

'I suppose so. Just don't put it all over Facebook,

Mam. Auntie Gwyneth will show it off at Christmas and make me look stupid.'

'Oh tosh! No, she wouldn't. We'll make a pact to release it on your eighteenth birthday instead.'

Emlyn frowned. His mam wasn't lying.

'Can I go now?' he asked politely.

'Fine. But do me a favour? I put a load of washing in the machine last night. Peg it on the line for me? Derek the weatherman says it'll be cold out, but dry today.'

Emlyn nodded and slipped from the bed.

'You're a good boy, Em. I love you.'

'You too,' he said, slipping away.

There were things he needed to do. School to prep for. Books to read. Summer was almost over. He wanted to salvage every spare minute of it.

Four

After saying her name repeatedly – the syllables so precious to her, now that she remembered them – Fanny focused her attention on her surroundings.

'How?' she wondered, feeling a tremor in her middle. She glanced at her hands: transluscent and white as starlight. She could see the bell on the cabinet quite clearly through her skin.

Definitely dead.

And she'd been somewhere else for an exceptionally long time. She knew that too.

The room was familiar now, but some of its objects... not so much. The small black box, for example, with a surface that reflected light almost like the skin of a lake. It looked rigid on its small table, with a similar coal-black device at its side, covered in raised numbers.

Fanny admired the ceiling next. It was low. And as she crossed the room to the bed – larger than she recalled – a rush of swirling imagery battered her mind, presenting her with memories of herself, lying flat on her back and staring at the ceiling above, her brow prickling with sweat and her body heaving with aches and pains.

'My room...' she uttered in painful realisation, staring at the lily-patterned bell with woeful eyes, '... at the inn. These were my quarters.'

Then.

How cruel, she raged inwardly. To have died and dreamt in her last moments that she might be reunited with her family one day, only to end up alone at the same bleak place that had brought her such misery. Had she done nothing good in life to rescue herself from despair and loneliness?

In a swish of skirts – the same outfit she had worn day in and day out as she carried out her duties as a maid – she stomped over to the door, passing through the wood in a sensation of cold abruptness, like opening your front door to a biting, frosty morning. She passed other doors on her right in a hurry, and met with a bright light that beamed from the staircase and hallway below. Far too bright to be candles.

On the bottom step, she paused. There was a woman with a cloth, dusting a ledge. She was curvy and dark haired, with an apron tied at her waist.

'Oh! A maid,' Fanny cried out. 'Please! Good lady. Can you help me? What year is this? Can you tell me news of my sister? Is she coming for me? Oh, please!

I need your help.' Her hands brushed the woman's shoulder as she reached for her in desperation. But the stranger remained unmoved, humming to herself as she ran the dust-caked cloth over the edges of hanging frames on the walls.

'You must help me,' Fanny tried again. 'I don't know why I'm here!'

'Malcolm?' the woman barked.

'Yeah?' came a distant response.

'Did you pick up more soy milk? In case we're invaded by vegans again?'

'Erm… I'll grab some after the dishwasher has done its cycle.'

The woman made a 'hmm' noise.

Fanny stamped her foot in frustration and eyed the exit, through another door into the main room. Furrowing her brow in determination, she took three steps forward and then halted as suddenly, something heavy clamped strong, invasive hands around her narrow waist.

'Well, well, well,' drooled a gravelly male voice as the grasping hands swivelled her around. The man's hulking presence filled the hallway. He gripped Fanny possessively, a toothy sneer forming on his face as she struggled to pull away. 'Hello, there, young lady. So, you're the one who woke me up with all that infernal noise, eh?' He gave a raspy chuckle, eyes burning like coals. 'I think you'd better go back upstairs, little lamb.' He leaned closer to her ear as she recoiled. 'I'm dying to hear your story…'

Five

Emlyn hadn't really made any close friends in Llanvihangel Crucorney Primary. In a world of young boys wanting to be football stars and wrestling champions, he instead wanted to be the next Roald Dahl or Charles Dickens. This made him weird. The weird boy who lived in a weird home.

Though he heard the occasional murmur of the word 'weird', Emlyn was never really bullied. The other children in his class let him get on with his writing in his little black leather notebook, without passing comment. Except one time. Michael Cleaver had asked – when collecting a ball that had rolled close to Emlyn's foot – 'Are you writing about school?' To which Emlyn replied, 'I'm writing about everything.'

The question on Emlyn's lips, the morning of his first day at comprehensive, was: would his new school like him?

Maybe this time would be different. Maybe there would be kids just like him that he could hang out with at break time. (Not that he expected there to be others living in, or around, haunted inns. But you get the idea). Maybe the library was fat and juicy with books of every subject and size, leaving him spoiled for choice. Maybe, instead of running laps during PE, they'd let him read in a patch of sunlight to rest his legs, because his long limbs hated exercise. And maybe in assemblies, the seating wouldn't be alphabetical – meaning he'd be well away from Osian Jenson, who farted a lot.

Emlyn's mam took the photographs she so desperately wanted of him in his crisp uniform and pecked him on the head outside the school – though luckily from inside their beaten-up car and not in public for all to spy. He was also grateful the beaten-up car had four wheels – not three, like his dad had originally wanted from the second-hand car place on the outskirts of Abergavenny. That would have been even worse than living in a haunted inn.

'Keep your mobile turned off and concentrate in class. But if you do get a chance at lunchtime, send me a text to let me know you're okay,' his mam pestered.

Emlyn realised in that moment that he'd left his mobile at his bedside. Though many kids had them glued to their hands, ears or pockets, he didn't often use his. In fact, he was pretty sure it wasn't even turned on, as he hadn't charged it for ages. Something about the tiny glowing screen gave him a headache. And other than his mam, he had no one to talk to.

'If I'm not busy, I will,' he lied, to avoid telling her he rarely carried around the iPhone she'd so cheerily bought him last Christmas.

'I'm proud of you, Em. And so's your dad.' She was tearing up. Time to get out of there.

'I know, Mam,' Emlyn said quickly and shut the car door with a creak of its hinges.

'*Hwyl!*' she yelled after him. They were a family of brief, unpractised Welsh, but Emlyn's mam insisted they try speaking it when they could. After all, the visitors at the Skirrid Inn – who often travelled from distant shores – might take away a piece of Wales with them in their hearts if they heard the occasional native word.

'*Hwyl,*' he shot back, as a group of youths made loud kissy noises at him. Obviously the 'goodbye affection' had not gone amiss by those in the general view of his parents' crummy vehicle. They smirked and pointed and giggled. One of them boldly waved at Emlyn's mam, who waved back with a smile, oblivious to the mockery.

Emlyn ignored the cluster of snickering kids and marched on.

Don't let it get to you. Don't let it get to you. New school. New day. New life.

The fresh arrivals gathered in the main hall, which

Emlyn had meandered towards based on a vague memory from a 'new-school' trip they'd had before the summer holidays. It had been daunting, he recalled, as he'd begged his brain to remember every footstep of the route. His memory served him well.

As he entered, his eyes darted towards the grey-haired wisp of a headmaster as he cried '*Croeso!*' to the masses.

Emlyn stood with his bag on one shoulder, perspiring at the edge of the crowd as names were barked out by their designated teachers. He wished it was as glamourous as Hogwarts: an old wizard's 'sorting' hat singing boisterously, filling hearts with hope and ease, followed by the individual announcement of student houses. But this was more of a cluttery-clattery mish-mash of shuffling and coughing and rustling and pushing to the front, joining queues of giddy, hyped-up lads and lasses.

It wasn't long before the form tutors took their new charges to classrooms that were nowhere near as colourful as their previous primary schools. Some of the year seven students were chatty. Others kept their eyes down – clutching new rucksacks with pencil cases rattling inside – and walking along alien corridors in squeaky, fresh-from-the-store shoes. The unknown swallowed them like a hungry beast, drowning them all with random staircases, unfamiliar rooms, shiny buffed floors, distant toilet stops and students that seemed to get taller and taller and taller.

Emlyn ran his fingers beneath his shirt collar when he was at last seated in his form room – the room he would meet for registration until the end of his comprehensive school days – and, with a pang of embarrassment, felt something solid there. As he worked it free with his index finger, the cardboard that supported the collar's shape popped out onto the table.

'Ha!' A boy nearby choked on laughter. 'Didn't your mam remember to get all the cardboard out from between your clothes?'

'Guess not,' Emlyn laughed half-heartedly. At least the cardboard proved his clothes were new and not second-hand, he thought, red-faced.

'What an idiot!' the kid guffawed, as Emlyn swiped the offending cardboard onto the floor and kicked it away from his chair. He was painfully aware that the boy who had seen the whole thing was now melodramatically retelling it to friends who, during private moments, checked they hadn't made the same mistake.

That was the first incident where Emlyn had felt ridiculous. The second came at lunchtime when he was about to take a seat in the food hall. He could have eaten his packed lunch outside, but he had yet to discover a quiet spot. Instead, he gravitated towards the tinkling and bustling of the canteen. As he'd made to sit, an older boy on the nearest table had pulled the seat from beneath him. Emlyn landed hard on the wooden floor, his elbow striking awkwardly and sending his funny bone into an angry spasm. He shot up as quick as he could – before all the faces could turn and laugh – and rounded on his attacker.

'Not funny!' he growled at the boy, seething and puffing his chest.

''Ark at him. He's got fire in his belly!' The boy laughed to his friends and nudged a smirking girl to his left.

A dinner lady wandered over in her mint green uniform. She made a point of haughtily picking up the chair that Emlyn had left lying on the floor as he stormed from the hall. He noticed students from his old primary school on exiting, but none motioned him over or asked if he was okay. Their eyes were full of embarrassment. Confusion.

Sullen and hungry, Emlyn entered the school outer grounds – chill, with early signs of autumn. He ate his sandwiches leaning against a fence, his back to the school and his face staring beyond his confinement. He was just having a bad day, he decided. The older kids were acting up because summer was over and they had important exams ahead of them. Things would settle.

An Aero helped take the edge off with its chocolatey goodness, but with a sigh, Emlyn realised he still had a whole half-hour to kill before lunch ended. A half-hour in the wilds of the playground – so full of kids and yet such lonely terrain. He felt like the weakest pack member. The wolf with the gammy leg that could easily be picked off by predators. He just wanted to blend in somehow. To go unnoticed and unbothered. To be a ghost.

He plucked up the courage to ask for some guidance when his legs finally took him in a random direction (the longer he stood still, the more miserable he felt). A gentleman in a purple tie, whom Emlyn assumed was a teacher, gave him directions to the school's library. This was where he belonged. And after numerous wrong turns, he found it.

CLOSED UNTIL FURTHER NOTICE

A sign in red marker was taped against a set of inviting double doors. The pen had bled into the paper, making the letters bubble and spread. Through the slivers of glass, he could make out shelves with books stacked. A trolley with neglected novels. The lights were off inside.

Emlyn slid down the wall in defeat.

He glanced at his watch.

Fifteen minutes to go.

I'll read in the corridor, he decided and pulled out a book – his sanctuary.

The sound of someone clearing their throat suddenly made him drop his precious paperback onto his leg.

'Year seven? First day?' asked a woman in a long grey skirt and white blouse. Her hair was long and coiled like oily snakes, gathered at her neck in a scrunchy.

'Erm. Yes, Miss.'

'Shouldn't you be outside enjoying the dry weather? Making friends?'

Emlyn located his paperback and gripped it tight. The words *I don't know how* were on the tip of his tongue, but he swallowed them in a heavy lump. Why was it he could talk to the tourists at the inn and not kids his own age? I mean, how would he even start the conversation? Hey, do you like *James and the Giant Peach*? How about an inn full of dead sheep thieves that were thrown from the banister and hanged? No? Oh. Okay! See you round then. We should do lunch sometime!

'What are you reading?' the teacher continued, when Emlyn's speechless behaviour left an awkward silence.

'Oh. Um. *Spellfall*. Katherine Roberts.' He flashed her the cover.

'Hmm. Looks good,' she said, glancing at it quickly. 'Well... the library is closed for a couple of days. Something leaked through the roof and caused damaged during the summer.'

'Oh. That's sad,' Emlyn mumbled.

'You really should be outside,' she urged, but something about the wash of disappointment in Emlyn's eyes must have stalled her. 'You can read here just this once, seeing as its almost registration anyhow.'

'Thank you,' he enthused.

She nodded and left him to his reading, but not before turning back to say, 'The library will be a good place to make friends, if you find you're unsteady on your feet in the playground. Why not ask about being an assistant? There'll be openings now the older kids have left.'

Emlyn brightened. An assistant? At the library? What a wonderful idea! If only he could make it so.

He smiled as he read in peace.

The horizon was suddenly glowing with possibility after all.

Six

Fanny shuddered and let out a little whine as the hulking brute at her side ran a hand through her long brown hair.

'There now,' he said. 'Comfortable?' He had led her to a rose-patterned sofa in the next room, which was much larger than her own.

Fanny sniffed and wiped her nose with a rag she'd found tucked in an apron pocket. A string of pearly ectoplasm came away from her nostril and dripped from the cloth, landing on the floor. It was foul and fascinating all at once, but she was too scared to give it any more acknowledgement.

'Those vile guests will be up shortly, in search of a show. So, let us not dally with our introductions. I'm George Jeffreys. Judge Jeffreys to you. And your name, my dear, is…?'

Judge Jeffreys. This made sense to Fanny. The man was wearing a hideous wig, with layers of tight white curls that dangled over broad shoulders. His heavy-looking robes were black as an ocean at night. His face was wrinkled around cruel eyes and his sharp chin was coated in a day's growth of hair.

'Fanny,' she replied, curtly.

'Hmm. Fanny. Well. It's extraordinary that a beautiful maiden such as yourself should appear so abruptly in a house full of dead thieves.' He spat the last word. 'What are your ties to this place?'

Fanny glanced around the room with skittish eyes. The four-poster bed, the elegant chair by a dressing table laden with trinkets, the grand wardrobes: none of these items had been present when she had been alive. The building had altered, undoubtedly, but her spirit felt the same foreboding emanating from the walls surrounding her, just as she had when cleaning her master's boots, or scrubbing the floors, or cooking the evening meal in a stifling kitchen.

And all that work for a meagre handful of coins each month that she could send back to –

'Girl! Speak up!' Judge Jeffreys barked. He was not a patient man. The men condemned to death in his courtroom had always been dealt with swiftly. An assertive thump of his gavel against polished wood and the jabbing of a gnarled finger saw to it that necks were laced in rope and bodies thrown to their end.

Such power.

He missed it.

'I worked here!' she explained hurriedly. 'A maid. I died, in my quarters. Consumption, the master said. He let me waste to bones in my bed. He promised he'd get a letter to my sister –'

'Where have you been all these years?' the judge questioned, cutting her off.

Fanny shook her head, trying to shake the memory of where she'd been – what she called the Grey Place. But what was worse, she wondered: a realm where memories faded and emptiness enfolded her, or a world where a man in black robes stroked her hair as if she were his pet?

'The between,' she murmured. 'A place with no colour or hope. Just an unfeeling, cold existence.'

The Judge snarled. 'Purgatory.'

'Excuse me, sir?'

'Purgatory. The place where the dead go to wait before it is decided if they should embrace heaven, or fall to the pits of hell...'

'But I did nothing wrong!' she protested.

'This is one judgement I cannot make, for it is God above that will decide your fate.' He stroked her hair, even as she cowered away. 'Something brought you back here, my dear. You've been waiting for someone. Or something. It seems to me that your business at the Skirrid Inn remains unfinished.'

Seven

'Can I have the keys, Mam?' Emlyn asked later that evening from the living-room doorway. She lifted her head from where she lay nestled in the crook of his dad's arm. They were on the sofa watching *Top Gear*. His dad liked it for the cars. His mam liked it for the jokes. It was one of their favourite things to watch together on nights the inn was closed to the public.

'Don't you have any homework to do?' she asked suspiciously.

'After the first day?' Emlyn replied, as if this were a dumb question.

'I don't know if it's a good idea. One of the menu boards on the wall fell off. But I can't see how. It's been tightly screwed in! The whole thing just came crashing to the floor when I was vacuuming this morning. Scared the life out of me!'

Emlyn was unimpressed. He knew what she was implying because his mam put anything and everything down to ghosts. Misplaced hairbrush? Ghosts. Forgotten ten-pound note in the washing machine? Ghosts. One egg broken in a pack of ten?

Ghosts. Dirty footprints on the floor in the shape of Dad's boots? Messy ghosts.

'He can go in, Maur,' his dad announced, pressing the volume button on the remote so he could hear the roar of engines better. 'It'll be fine.'

Emlyn took the keys from the pot before his mam could protest, leaving the house in a hooded jumper, his notebook and pen to hand. Some nights, like this one, he would open the Skirrid and lock himself inside for a few hours. Just to get away. He somehow felt disconnected from the real world when he was there by himself, which he preferred. He could write better. Think more clearly.

On the third floor, the stairs came to a landing with a sofa and an array of really old cobwebs that had been left there for decoration. His mam had threatened to suck them up with the vacuum cleaner, but his dad had argued it made the building creepier for the guests.

And creepy was exactly what guests came for, after all. As long as the cobwebs didn't touch Emlyn's skin, he didn't mind them being there. He pictured, in years to come when he was a famous author, articles written in the paper about his childhood – the lonely boy and his inn; master of spiders and of waking shadows! He'd tell the world he got his inspiration from the dark and –

A sudden noise broke his concentration.

He'd been doodling in the back of his notebook – pen scratching at the page in little intricate swirls – when something had caught his attention. A sort of sob?

He shook his head. Convinced himself it was a car. Or someone walking outside. As much as he craved a world like the ones in his favourite books (the Shire in *The Lord of the Rings*, for example. Now there was a place he could happily live out his days), there was always an explanation for things that went bump in the night at Skirrid Inn.

He focused on his notebook again. Bits of a poem came to him, about a girl who planted a book instead of a seed and a tree of pages sprang from the ground, crisp white with black, type-written words. He decided it would be a picture book and broke it up into verses as he went –

That noise again.

Almost like a coughing this time. Distant.

Beneath the sleeves of his jumper, the hair on his arm was standing at attention. Sure, it wasn't the first time he'd been startled by a noise whilst alone at the inn, but it had always turned out to be something silly, like a tap left trickling in the kitchen (Dad!) or the wind outside playing havoc with the old walls and windows.

The noise petered out. All returned to silence.

Weird.

He carried on writing his verses, smiling at the bits he liked and feverishly scribbling out words he deemed imperfect. His head was noisy with characters dancing to his tune and he'd managed to produce four verses he was happy with before being disturbed yet again.

'Right, that's it!' he complained, closing his notebook. Somehow, speaking the words aloud made him less nervous.

The strange sobbing was very faint, but loud enough for him to notice. And worry. There was not a doubt in his mind: someone had to be outside the inn – probably using the Skirrid's bench to rest – perhaps with arms wrapped around themselves, mumbling into the crooks and folds of their jacket?

But as Emlyn crept down onto the second level, his thoughts were swayed.

The sobbing became louder. Stopping and starting. Stopping and starting.

His heart did an unexpected flip flop.

But surely… no… in all his years… he had never once been convinced that it could be a –

Gently he pressed his ear to the door of Room One.

Nothing.

Nothing.

Sob. Sniff.

His head snapped quickly in the direction of Room Three.

You're just tired, his mind reasoned in haste. *Think logically*!

He'd never been freaked out before. Never. The inn was a safe-haven. And now he was starting to feel unnerved beyond comprehension. He didn't like it.

Slowly, he took two steps backwards, feeling for the banister.

Whatever was going on, he didn't want to stick around. His heart was racing. Sweat prickled on his forehead and the back of his neck.

Go get the key to Room Three, his brain enticed him. *See for yourself. It could be a forgotten guest locked in there*! The old doors were very thick and the noises within, muffled. Someone could be hurt.

Sob. Sniff. Sob, sob.

He bit his lip and, as quietly as he could, made his way to the ground floor. He collected the key and paused at the bottom of the stairs to listen closely.

Sob.

Sob.

Then –

'Oh, Emily. I've failed you! I'm so sorry, my sweet girl.'

Emlyn gasped in fright at the strangely garbled words of distress.

Oh my... oh gosh, oh... oh Lord! I'm freaking out, his mind raved. His body sparked into flight-mode, leaping for the front door, the keys to Room Three abandoned on the bar top with a slamming of his hand. He fumbled with the lock, desperate for the cool night air and freedom to enfold him.

But there came an almighty SHRIEK that sent him dropping to the floor – arms folded over his face in terror.

Eight

Silence.

He listened to the heavy intakes of his own rapid breathing and waited. When he was sure the noises – the shrieks – were over, he lifted his head cautiously and peered over his arms. The inn was as it should be: still. Quiet. Empty.

He grabbed his notebook and pen from the flagstone floor and left, almost forgetting to lock everything up behind him. He did so with swift, yet wobbling hands, anxious to create some distance between himself and the building.

'That was quick,' his dad commented from the sofa on Emlyn's return. His mam was asleep with her head on his dad's lap, the hint of a snore gurgling in her nose and throat.

'Yeah. I got hungry. Fancied a snack. Didn't want to make a mess of the inn's kitchen,' Emlyn lied, heading for their 'house' kitchen with plans to make himself a slice of toast and a cup of sweet tea. His hands were still shaking and he needed a distraction from the freaky noises rattling in his memory.

He couldn't drink his tea quick enough, ignoring the sting when the hot liquid touched his tongue.

His brain became congested with thoughts and fears. That shriek! It had sounded so human. And there had been a voice. Words. He tried to reason with himself: it was someone in a car. Or people – maybe teenagers, out walking dogs – messing around with one another on passing?

But the street had been vacant when he'd run home for safety's sake.

It came from inside the inn, and you know it, his mind argued.

I'm being ridiculous. I sound like a moronic tourist.
But Mam and Dad believe the dead are in there.

Draining the dregs of his mug, he debated telling his parents what he'd heard, but firmly decided the noises were nothing to worry about. If they went over to check out the commotion, there would be zero evidence of anyone in distress. And they'd just be annoyed with him for disrupting their evening off work.

Saying nothing's best.

When Emlyn's toast was devoured and the crumbs swiped into the dishcloth, he found his laptop in the comfort of his bedroom and clicked on the website that held the reviews and comments of those who had stayed at the Skirrid Inn. But there was no mention of a shriek in the night. One reviewer, however, mentioned the bell, which struck Emlyn as odd.

There hadn't been a bell on the premises until yesterday.

> *We heard little in the night besides the creaking of the boards beneath our feet and the radiators clunking at intervals. But there was one thing that startled us and could not be explained. A bell started ringing! We were all in Room One – talking – when we heard it. When we went to investigate, it had stopped. Perhaps the old maid had returned? We can only guess the bell's call was for her. But Room Three, the maid's alleged quarters, was empty. And on staying there, we heard and saw nothing. We soon went back to Room Two – the Judge's old court – where we found it unbearably cold and unsettling.*

Emlyn read the short review twice. The inn was said to house many ghosts. 'Hanging' Judge Jeffreys was the more commonly discussed spirit – stalking about in memory of his courtroom days. And then there were the men that Judge Jeffreys had sentenced to be hanged by the neck. They lingered too, apparently.

The maid wasn't someone Emlyn knew a great deal about. His mam and dad were always pressing the scarier, angrier ghosts onto the public. Though they were obviously aware of her, or they wouldn't have asked him to place a bell prop in Room Three.

Feeling almost embarrassed for using the internet to research his own home, he checked the available information on 'alleged ghosts' and recorded deaths at the inn. There was plenty on the Judge. Even a creepy photo of a painting of him in his robes, with brown puffy hair. There was also mention of an 'exceptionally bloody period' around 1685 (*ych a fi!*), which gave Emlyn the chills. But then, with roving eyes that absorbed the type on his glowing laptop screen, he read about a spirit that wasn't remotely criminal or malevolent.

The maid girl.

Fanny Price.

She was aged thirty-five when she'd died of consumption in what was now Room Three.

Rumour had it, the bell was to call her to her chores.

And this time maybe... just maybe... she'd answered.

Nine

After their talk of purgatory and unfinished business, Judge Jeffreys had settled into telling Fanny about some of his more interesting criminal cases at the inn. He spoke with gusto and passion, relishing the parts where men were destroyed at his request, the slamming of the gavel sending thieves to their doom.

It terrified Fanny to the core.

At intervals, the Judge would chuckle and then slip a hand through Fanny's hair, mumbling about how he wished he could really feel its softness. He'd tell her she had a fine chin and delicate eyelashes. How he longed to see the true colour of her eyes.

Fanny was repulsed by his words.

That evening, the Inn's living guests stationed themselves in Room One. Jeffreys had hoped for a silent night, but was enraged when he soon found himself torn from admiring Fanny's upturned nose.

A growl escaped deep in the cavern of his throat.

'Pesky, pompous, imbecilic meddlers!' He jumped up from his seat and stomped around the room, arms waving and robes rustling. 'They come here and call my name as if to mock me! So many of them, in disrespectful droves! Useless men and excitable ladies in ridiculous outfits. There were never as many as this before! I could sleep for years at a time! And now, I have to bury my head in stone just to drown out their voices.'

'Who are they?' Fanny managed to squeak out, when his ranting had slowed.

'Guests of this wretched inn. They pay a sum of money to sit in these rooms and talk to the dead.'

Fanny lifted a hand to her mouth. 'You mean... us?'

'So they think,' he spat in disgust. 'And it's as if their presence gives me energy. The more of those flesh-sacks that wander this place, the more frazzled and unhappily whole I feel. Hungry. Always hungry. Restless. Uncomfortable. Heavy. Like I have weights on my feet dragging me into the earth. It's infuriating.'

'Can you not just leave here? Escape them?'

His eyes sparked. 'Can you?'

Fanny hadn't tried. Yet. But something in his tone suggested it would be a fruitless endeavour.

'I wouldn't go getting your hopes up, maid. Whatever brought you back, I'm afraid it is unlikely you'll reverse it now. You'll be caught here with me.' He grinned, showing his dirty teeth. 'Forever.'

Suddenly, a door opened.

A man leading a small crowd of people entered the room, filling the corners with static energy that only the dead could sense.

Fanny jumped to her feet and shuffled away from the living; all their bright clothing and unruly hairstyles offended her eyes. Had so much changed, since the Grey Place had taken her hostage?

'This is Room Two,' the man announced, 'said to be the court of Judge Jeffreys...' The Judge bared his teeth at the invaders and thumped a fist against the post of the four-poster-bed. It made a gentle *thunk* that silenced the crowd instantly.

'Did you...?'

'Shh!'

Fanny took the unexpected drove of ghost hunters in the room as her chance to leave, immersing herself in wall and shadows, until her spirit found its way into her quarters. She sat on a bed so unlike her old one, and wept loudly into her hands.

* * *

Fanny wasn't sure how much time had passed. She hadn't taken much notice of the sun rearing above the mountains outside, or the way it moved across the sky in a lazy crawl. She hadn't even lifted her head when the guests at the inn had pushed their way into her room that evening, to sit on the bed and listen to the nothingness around them. Her memories were trickling back to her and she pieced them together with an ache in her chest.

She had come to the inn to work. Because her sister needed help. She could picture her sister's face. The long chestnut hair and hazel eyes. The smattering of freckles. The way her body had filled out so suddenly, announcing she was no longer a girl but a woman with questions and aspirations.

She needed my help, Fanny thought. But the rest of the memory was a swirling mass, drifting out of reach. Scrunching up her brow and nose, she prayed for answers. Prayed with all her might.

Why had she gone to the inn to work? So far from home? Her family?

'Mamma died,' she whimpered to herself, suddenly.

A vision exploded of her mam's cold, wide-eyed face on a winter's day. Found with her basket empty and trodden on. The town's folk had discovered her in the lane, tossed over the dry-stone wall like she was cattle; foxes had already gotten at her throat.

No one had come forward with evidence. There were no witnesses. No explanation for her sad end.

Mamma was buried on a hill, in view of their little cottage. Next to their father's grave.

'It's my fault,' Emily had sobbed.

'Oh, hush now,' Fanny comforted her sister, grey-faced with sorrow.

She could see it all in waves of coloured memory now. The fireplace crackling with warmth. The rationed logs, neatly stacked. The bread they'd savoured, though their stomachs twisted with hunger and sorrow – picking tiny crumbs and rolling them around their tongues, before swallowing them with effort.

'It is,' Emily insisted, lifting her tear-filled eyes to Fanny.

'You can't blame yourself for something a heartless traveller likely did.'

'Mamma didn't want anyone to know!' Emily continued. 'She was going to hide it. Hide me. And when the baby came, she would say she found it in the woods and take the brunt of the town's questions. She was afraid. She said to me: Emily, their resentment will be fierce. A young girl. No husband. A babe in her arms. They'll hate you for your sins. We have to lie.' The tears started to pour from Emily's eyes. 'She didn't want that for me. But I did this to her. I deserve to be spat on.'

'What on earth are you talking about?' Fanny rasped, her veins icy, though the fire flickered nearby.

Emily cried harder behind splayed fingers.

'I'm having a baby!' Her hand reached for her abdomen that was indeed a little puffy under her blouse, now that her fingers traced its shape.

Fanny was paralysed.

Emily took this to be anger.

'Oh, please, don't hate me, sister,' she begged, reaching for Fanny's skirts and grasping them with all her worth. 'You're all I have now. You're all I have…'

Fanny was brought back to the reality of her room at the Skirrid, where she sat huddled in a corner with her knees to her chest. Night had fallen again. So quickly. So cold.

'Oh, Emily. I've failed you! I'm so sorry, my sweet girl,' she moaned loudly. 'What became of you, my love?'

As tears of ectoplasm rolled down her cheeks, splashing onto the wooden beams, her body jolted.

Something stirred before her.

'What. Is. All. This. NOISE? On our night of peace, I should add!' bellowed the Judge, his body emerging from the wall with an offensively bright glow. He stormed over, filling the room with his great shoulders, and as he grabbed Fanny by the nape of her neck – lifting her so her feet dangled – she let out an ear-shattering shriek.

Ten

'Have a good day,' Emlyn's mam called from the window, before the car chugged off in a cloud of exhaust fumes.

Another day in paradise, Emlyn thought sarcastically.

He hadn't slept much – dreaming of sobs and shrieks and unexplainable voices. Bunching his pillow up around his ears to drown out the night, he'd eventually slept with his headphones in – making use of an old iPod his dad had given him, full of Meat Loaf and Stereophonics albums – to calm his speedy heart. Sleep at last engulfed him around midnight, but before he could dream of something soothing and wonderful, his robot alarm clock had screamed and lifted a whirring arm on the bedside table, eyes flashing red.

Emlyn got through most of the school morning with minimal trouble. He managed a few 'hellos' to students at his classroom tables and felt relatively uplifted by their smiles of acknowledgment – until the afternoon break arrived.

He was leaving a graffiti-riddled toilet cubicle in search of a sink when he felt something large collide with his shoulder. A yelp escaped his mouth automatically, and he shrivelled on realising the shadow lingering over him was that of a much older boy. This particular boy was flanked by two others. All of them brown-haired and all fierce-looking with against-regulation-loosely-knotted-ties.

'Someone told me about you. You're the creepy kid,' said the boy who had knocked into Emlyn with precise force. He had a menacing authority and stood like a figure on an action movie poster, chin up and defiant.

Emlyn kept his head low and quickly began washing his hands. There was no soap left in the dispenser, so he made a point of squelching his hands together under the tap water as best he could, focusing only on this and not the daunting presence of bodies nearby.

'You live in a haunted house, right?' the closest boy continued.

'Not exactly,' Emlyn said quietly, moving towards the hand dryer. Maybe if he treated the situation casually, he would become as calm as he pretended to be. But these boys, certainly, were the same tricksy crowd that had tripped him in the dinner hall, for all to laugh and mock him, on his first day.

'That makes you a right weirdo,' the boy jibed.

Emlyn rubbed his still-damp hands on the thighs of his charcoal-coloured trousers and turned to leave.

The three boys huddled closer around him, the collective smell of lunch on their tangy breaths.

'So, have you seen anything?' one asked, poking Emlyn in the shoulder.

'No,' he replied.

'What? Nothing at all?'

'I haven't,' he said, deadpan now. He wasn't about to open up to them about weird shrieks in the night. They were the last people that needed further reason to pester him.

'Then your parents are lying about their so-called ghosts. They're making money off innocent people. Scumbags.'

Emlyn frowned and leapt to his parents' defense. 'We can't change the history of the place. If people say they've seen things and other customers want to see it for themselves, it's not lies. It's curiosity.'

'Oooh, listen to posh-pants,' laughed the tallest of the three. In a high-pitched voice, he mimicked: 'It's curiosity!'

'I'm curious about this,' said one of them. He had a smudge of something tomatoey in the corner of his lips. Puree perhaps, from canteen ham and pineapple pizza. The boy tried to snatch Emlyn's rucksack off his shoulder, but before he could grab it, Emlyn rammed into them. They scattered to the side like bowling pins whacked by a ball and glowered after Emlyn as he escaped through the door.

He barrelled straight into a dark-haired girl with a bob cut and starry rucksack, who gasped and cried out, 'Hey!'

Emlyn righted himself and ran away from her disgruntled expression. All he could focus on was the sound of the word 'freak' ringing loudly against the walls of the boys' toilets as it was shouted after him in his wake.

Eleven

Emlyn – downtrodden by school bullies and mind-boggled by new school homework – had not set foot inside the Skirrid since the night of the shriek.

But.

His mam insisted that she required his help with their paranormal-investigating guests. That she simply could *not* do the evening shift without him. And that she would add an extra book to his monthly order for disturbing his post-school peace, in which he planned on prodding at school textbooks and moping in bed with the duvet dragged over his wilting frame.

Emlyn had firmly kept his promise to mention nothing of the shriek to anyone, even though it replayed in his head over and over, making his belly lurch. It had made sleeping difficult at night; he jumped at every noise. Realising he couldn't go on like that any longer, he'd lugged his old cassette player from beneath the bed and blown the dust off an audio book version of *The Lion, The Witch and The Wardrobe*. The old whirring tape was perfect for softly playing in the background of his frenzied mind until Emlyn was drowsy enough to turn it off without leaving the comfort of his blanket-nest.

The reason his mam needed him so fervently at the inn was because his dad happened to be away at a rare, organised game of five-a-side football with friends at the town leisure centre. It was a gathering of old buddies from school and once a year they made a point of giving up their daily routines as family men to kick a ball around – generally exhausting themselves before going home to crash on their beds where, the following day, they would wake suffering the aches of forgotten youth, and wondering why they hadn't just watched a match together on the television instead.

So, this left Emlyn at his mam's disposal.

'The guests have almost finished their meals,' she said as he wandered up to the bar. It was busy. The locals were filling the main social room and the guests were shoulder-to-shoulder in the dining area. Denise, their part-time barmaid – employed since the influx of visitors – was clinking glasses into the dishwasher, trying to keep up with the mounting pile of dirties in the tray she had used to briskly gather them.

'You'll have to do the tour for me,' his mam instructed. 'The kitchen is a mess and I need Denise out here. Everyone seems to want a meal tonight. Local takeaway must be closed.' She huffed strands of loose hair from her red face.

'Seriously?' Emlyn complained, aghast. The very idea of doing the tour made him sweat. He wasn't a confident person when it came to crowds. She knew that. What if he forgot something? Or got something wrong? Or tripped over a guest? 'Can't I go on the pumps? Pull pints? Take orders?'

His mam frowned. 'And have the police walk in to see a minor selling alcohol to men and women three times his age? Don't be so ridiculous! Come on, boyo. You want to be a writer, yes? It'll be good practice for when you become a published author. You'll have no choice but to talk in public then! Do it for me, just this one night. Don't forget that extra paperback I promised you in return...' She waggled her eyebrows up and down.

'I barely remember the stories, Mam. And what if I can't answer a question?'

'There's nothing to it,' she said, taking money from a gentleman and turning to the till. Her voice carried over her shoulder in the manner of someone reeling off a boring shopping list. 'Devil's tankard, Judge Jeffreys, 182 hanged victims. The old beam, etcetera, etcetera. Once you start talking, it'll all come back to you!'

'Fanny the maid?' he asked. The words felt heavy in his mouth.

'Yes, and Fanny, of course. Show them the bell I bought! And don't forget to show them the old cell where they kept the criminals. Your father always forgets that part. I swear he thinks I've just put the vacuum cleaner and mop in there for storage, but it's still vastly important.'

Emlyn scowled and drew up his hood, blocking out the pub for a moment. A group of men perched on bar stools were starting at him now. Waiting for him to make a fool of himself, he was sure. Of all the things he could help his mam with, why the tour?

I am so not cool with this, he thought dismally.

'Stand up straight and pull that hood down!' His

mother's voice broke into his melancholy. She handed a customer his change and moved swiftly on to refilling the next empty glass. 'Give me five minutes to get the tables cleaned up and you can take them upstairs.'

Emlyn sighed. At least, he figured, with so many people around, he wasn't likely to hear anything too creepy. And he wished profoundly that he could return to those times he wasn't spooked by the inn, when the hauntings had been just a joke to him.

Am I admitting that there truly is something here? After all these years of disbelief?

He sulked in the corner, ignoring the teasing voice in his head, until his mam summoned him. He stood at her side wearing his best false smile while she introduced him to the waiting ghost hunters in a booming voice. They all nodded their hellos. There were six of them – four women and to men, all somewhere between thirty and forty years of age – with their cheeks rosy and bellies full of a hot meal on a cold night. They looked almost garden gnome-like in appearance, minus the pointy red hats.

'They have their keys,' his mam muttered in an aside. 'On with the show!'

There was a brief silence as the excited group calmed in wait.

'Hi,' Emlyn greeted, with a curt wave. For extra points from his mam, he added, 'And *croeso*.'

'Now, if you have any questions, my son Emlyn will be happy to answer them. So, sleep tight everyone. Or not.' She winked at her audience and then bustled out of the dining room, already thinking about the dishes that needed scrubbing in the kitchen.

'Okay. Follow me, everyone,' Emlyn said, leading the way. He feared a bad online review, for which his mam would without doubt scold him, so he forced himself into a perky, upbeat tone. He hoped it was convincing. Inside, he felt fragile with the pressure – his palms were moist with liquid worry.

Their first stop was at the bottom of the stairs.

'This,' he pointed upwards at a beam with the new, novelty hangman's noose fixed to it, 'is the very same beam where the original noose was tied.' He stretched and ran his hands over the grooves, feeling his top untuck from his trousers to reveal a strip of pale skin. Quickly, he fumbled to cover it up. 'You can feel here where the rope bit into the wood, wearing it down over time with each new victim that was hanged by the neck.'

The group took it in turns to trace their fingers over the marks, shuddering and murmuring, grinning and smirking.

Emlyn showed them the old cell, as per his mam's request – icy, with barely any legroom. He then moved on to the main bedrooms, where he started to feel a bit more confident. He encouraged each person with their designated keys to open the big, heavy doors in turn.

'On two occasions, we've had the keys break like butter in the locks,' Emlyn recalled, as an eager couple turned their key. They were fitting it into the keyhole together, like lovers cutting a cake at their wedding, whilst giggling excitably. Emlyn felt it was time to quash the group's giddiness with a reminder of the inn's grisly reputation.

'So, in this room, some have claimed to experience the sensation of being robbed of air. Choked by something or someone at their throats. Lots of guests have mentioned it. Some have even left in the middle of the night because it scared them so much.'

One of the guests murmured an 'ooh'.

Another touched their neck surreptitiously beneath the collar of a dark shirt.

'It must be horrible, choking and not being able to push away the thing that's causing it…'

The other guests murmured agreement as they moved onto the second room, where Emlyn felt himself floundering for information. Desperately, he tried to recall the stories about Room Two, but all his brain supplied was panic: *You're messing up! You're messing up! Mam will be seriously disappointed if you don't pull this off!*

'It's much colder in here, by far!' one of the group observed, the words slicing through Emlyn's repetitive thoughts.

'Yes, I noticed that as soon as I walked in,' agreed one of the women. She had grey roots showing through auburn hair and a happy face that showed signs of wrinkles around her eyes.

They all discussed the dramatic drop in temperature, which wasn't the first time Emlyn had heard this. Room Two tended to be cooler, but his parents had never located the source of the draught. Inevitably, the cold was said to be linked to spiritual activity. His parents neither confirmed nor encouraged this. It was the reviews online that kept the rumours strong.

'Shall we move on to Room Three?' He directed everyone into the corridor again. 'This is the room where a housemaid named Fanny Price once spent her time, summoned by a bell to go about her chores. She died of –'

He heard a sob.

He froze.

'You okay, lad?'

He blinked quickly and shook his head a jot. 'She died of con –'

Sob.

He turned sharply to the door and stared at it.

The guests became visibly uncomfortable. One of them laughed in an awkward fashion.

'He's winding us up, right?'

'What is it?'

'Can you hear something?'

Emlyn placed his ear to the door, ignoring the group at his back waiting on an explanation. He strained to listen.

'*Leave me be!*' came a voice from the other side.

Sharp, with a static rasp.

Feminine.

Frightened.

Emlyn knocked into his audience, bumbling his way backwards in fear.

'Out of the way, let me listen!' enthused the guest with the red and grey hair, relishing the tension and putting her ear to the door breathlessly. One of the gentlemen nudged her aside, hurriedly putting the key in the lock to discover what had spooked their host so dramatically.

'Tell me what you heard!' demanded a man with

a navy jumper wrinkling around his middle. He scrambled to grip Emlyn's arm before the boy could make his escape.

'Are you tricking us?'

'Something's in there,' Emlyn choked out, shrugging him off. 'Let me go!'

Ignoring the man's protests, he pulled his jumper sleeve free and ran – down the staircase, beyond the busy bar, out through the front door and into the night.

Twelve

Fanny choked on words that wouldn't come.

Since she had left the Grey Place, Judge Jeffreys had tormented her constantly. His energy was at its ripest when plenty of guests wandered the halls, and when the bar beneath his feet teemed with people. So many vibrant lives packed under one roof made his transparent hands flicker just a little bit brighter, made connecting with the physical world just a little bit easier. His favourite game was to tip over Fanny's bell and smirk when its gentle tinkle summoned her back from wherever she'd been hiding.

The more frightened she looked, the more wicked his smile. Tonight, he was strong enough the she could practically feel his ragged fingernails catching in her hair. But as always when she tried to protest, the words wouldn't come. All she could manage were feeble noises that made her sound weak and pitiful.

'It's so much more pleasant having a young lady here to entertain me, instead of those filthy thieves,' the judge was telling her. 'They are little more than shadows, really; hardly any fun at all.'

Fanny's lower lip trembled. She had never seen the thieves he kept mentioning. Were they even real? Was the Judge raving about something from his past life – unaware that they were no longer a part of his present? At last, Fanny's fear pushed her to speak.

'Please, I want to rest. I feel... I feel drained. And broken.'

He grabbed her hand as she made to squirm away, sobbing like a stray dog caught in a storm.

'No. Talk to me,' he commanded.

'*Leave me be!*' she begged, the words rushing out in a single burst.

His lip curled in fury.

'How dare you speak to me in such a disrespectful manner!'

He struck her across the cheek, and she whimpered as his hand passed through her.

'Now you'll sit there and do as I say. A lady should know her place. This is my world. I own this building. I was here long before you. So, heed my words, lamb, or I'll see to it you'll wish you had never come back here.'

Fanny drew her knees to her chest and nodded, tears of ectoplasm rolling down her face and puddling on the floorboards.

Jeffreys hovered over her. 'Tell me a story.'

'I have none,' she said in the meekest of voices, her hands twisting in her lap.

He leant in closer. 'Make it up,' he hissed.

She didn't know where to begin. But then she thought of her sister Emily, and how when they were little, she would whisper softly into the night to help her sleep. Of crows that could speak and bring trinkets. Of mice that had found a way to milk cows in the morning so that the farmers didn't have to. Of fairies that lived in the rolling Welsh hills, polishing and protecting the eggs of sleeping dragons.

'Once upon a t... time...' she began, imagining it was for her sister instead of the nightmare-man before her.

*　*　*

The maid had not gone unnoticed.

' *– new arrival –*'

' *– soft spirit –*'

' *– is gentle –*'

' *– sad –*'

' *– has she seen the other side –?*'

' *– the Death Bringer wants her for a pet –*'

' *– lost lamb –*'

' *– poor lamb! –*'

The thieves vibrated with intrigue, hiding in the crevices of the inn's walls. They rarely surfaced – tiny orbs of energy immersed in stone and mortar. Sleeping fitfully.

Dreaming of their days in court; the sensation of the stiff, unrelenting rope at their necks. Tossed over the banister. Life choking from their flailing bodies.

They liked to be small and insignificant now. The very opposite to the hulking Death Bringer. Being small meant they could keep their distance. Sulk in shadow. Avoid further torment. Though from time to time, they gathered as one – a mass of orbs creating the shape of a single, able-bodied man. Working in unison, they roamed the halls of the Skirrid, on those rare occasions that the Death Bringer slumbered.

Like a caged animal, they paced.

Evaluating changes.

Looking for hope.

For peace.

The Death Bringer was pre-occupied with the wee lass that had entered their echoing realm. But when at last her bedtime story was over, he left her to mourn and the thieves gathered to watch curiously from afar.

' – *stronger than she realises* –'

' – *tears are heavy* –'

' – *hush now. She wilts* –'

With overlapping voices, clipped and wispy, they jabbered to one another, moving their shimmering human form across the second-floor landing.

There were guests in Room Two, chattering and chittering. They had a bottle of wine and half-empty glasses, huddled around a coffee table. Some were seated on the sofa. Some on the bed. Others were cross-legged on the cool floor.

But the living visitors did not amuse the thieves like they once had.

They were all the same now.

The same reactions. The same stories. The same excited presence. They came to muse over the failings of the thieves. They did not come to grieve for their sudden departures. They wanted to communicate. Some even mocked them with the warmth of alcohol in their bellies.

'– *quiet now* –'

'– *she sleeps* –'

'– *do not frighten her* –'

'– *we won't hurt the fair one* –'

Together, the thieves strode into Room Three, as light as moth wings in moonlight. They found the girl huddled in the corner, her head partially submerged in the wall as she slept. Her face was red with spilled tears, and the was floor damp.

The mass of thieves crouched down on one knee, examining the woman closely.

She did not stir.

'– *deserves better* –' they whispered in agreement, sad for the young maid.

Scooping her up into their arms, they gently carried her to the bed where they lay her down without a word. Though they had no energy for it, they mimicked tucking the duvet over her narrow frame and then carefully backed away from her.

'– *dream sweetly* –'

They gave her one last look of empathy and, in an explosion of orb light, scattered – back to the crevices that held them tight for the best part of their eternity.

Thirteen

'Emlyn? You up there?'

A familiar voice from the foot of the stairs brought Emlyn's head out from under his duvet. He stopped his audio book from playing just as the door to his room creaked open.

His dad looked positively exhausted. The bags under his eyes were heavier than usual, and his hair was stuck at odd angles to a forehead still damp with lingering sweat. So he'd survived the football match with his friends, then. But the look on his face was not one of tired happiness. It was concern.

'Your mam said you stormed out before she could get any sense from you? And that it's too busy to just leave Denise at the bar. Why didn't you pick up the phone when she rang?'

Emlyn had heard the house phone tingling away in the lounge, but had been utterly unwilling to retrieve it. All the fear and adrenaline – not to mention the effort it was taking to push the voices from the inn out of his head – had left Emlyn with a nasty headache.

He sat up in his bed now, face pale and pinched.

'What is it, boyo? You look terrible.'

Emlyn found this statement mildly amusing, considering his dad looked like he'd done a few rounds in a boxing ring. And lost.

'I finished the tour for Mam and wanted to get back to my homework, that's all,' he lied. But why? Why not just tell him what he'd heard? Maybe his dad could explain it.

His dad frowned. 'No one hurtles hell-for-leather from the inn to their homework. Especially not you. You're more of a lazy-walk, draw-no-attention-to-himself kind of guy.'

Emlyn rubbed the back of his neck and sighed. 'Okay. I guess… I thought I heard something weird,' he admitted, defeatedly. 'I freaked. Sorry. I shouldn't have run.'

His dad looked thoughtful. 'Hey, no one is blaming you for running if you were frightened…'

The words stung a little. Emlyn didn't like thinking of himself as weak. He'd gone forever without being afraid of his home and he'd thought that had made him better than some of the people that left the Skirrid completely freaked out. He couldn't make friends, but he could spend the night alone in a haunted inn. Until recently.

'It could have been one of the guests winding me up,' he suggested, putting on a brave face.

'Well, it could have. But I think you're sharp enough to know if they were.'

Emlyn contemplated this silently.

'I know this isn't your average upbringing,' his dad continued. 'And you've been strong and understanding and so amazing, Em. You really have. Even when your mam and I were stressing about expanding the business and dealing with the television crew.' He leant forward and placed a hand on Emlyn's shoulder. 'I couldn't ask for a more wonderful boy.' Emlyn shuffled on the bed, proud and embarrassed all at once.

'Anything that worries you – talk to me. If something scares you, run to me. Run to your mam. Either of us. Don't run away and face it alone. We love you too much.'

Father and son shared a smile, and Emlyn's dad reached down to ruffle Emlyn's hair with his sweaty hands, which thankfully broke the serious 'man-to-man' conversation vibe. It was rare for things to get so sincere between them. Emlyn's dad was the nonchalant joker in the family. The one that drifted through the house singing silly song lyrics while he did his chores. It was Emlyn's mam that went in for heart-to-hearts, always pestering him about his feelings. How are you feeling about big school, love? And: Anything worrying you, sweetheart? And Emlyn's personal favourite: What's going on in that head of yours when you're cooped up writing by yourself, lad?

'Honestly. I made a mistake, Dad,' Emlyn reassured him.

'Perhaps I shouldn't have let you read that Stephen King book at such a young age, eh?' his dad said with a wink.

Emlyn laughed and forced himself not to look at his wardrobe where *The Shining* lay buried in a shoe box, underneath a pile of crumpled clothes, only half-read. He'd told his dad he'd finished it – and to be fair, he probably would. Someday. Even if he couldn't handle the creepiness just yet.

'As long as you're okay,' Emlyn's dad finished. 'I'm going to shower.' He made a play at sniffing the damp patches of his T-shirt. 'I'm not going to lie, I'm ponging after that match.'

'I did wonder if a rat had died in the attic again...'

'Ger-off!' Dad chortled, leaving the room.

And though he'd ben cheered for a moment, Emlyn felt a wave of foreboding as he stared at the back of his dad, leaving him to face the quiet room alone.

Fourteen

Judge Jeffreys retired to his room in a foul and burning mood. The maid girl had been telling him stories, as per his request – and though her soft words had been juvenile in nature, he'd been enjoying himself thoroughly. That was, until those infernal house guests had bustled in and interrupted. Calling out their names! Playing with the lily-painted servant's bell, the constant clink of clapper against porcelain driving him mad. Fussing around on the bed and talking complete and utter nonsense about traces of spiritual 'light anomalies' that were clearly just dust particles in the air.

Enraged, the Judge had shoved Fanny to the ground and gone back to pace heavily through his own room, thinking thunderous thoughts.

'Will you never cease?' he roared, as the guests, moving on with the hunt, barged into his room. He turned sharply to face them and saw a gentleman remove a bottle of whisky from a satchel, taking a swig from the bottle's long neck.

The Judge hovered close by, intrigued by the sound

of the man's satisfied sigh, and he found himself longing for a taste of the fiery liquid.

'If I were alive for just one more hour, I'd quaff that whisky until the bottle was dry,' he growled jealously. 'Tis for men, not boys like you,' he hissed in the man's face. The man's eyes darted left and right in confusion, the tiny hair follicles on his pink skin standing to attention.

The Judge moved closer and closer, teeth clenched so tightly they would have made a grinding sound, if they could make any noise at all. He was all but nose-to-nose with the man, who gripped his bottle of whisky tighter.

'Guys…' he murmured to the group. 'It's really cold all of a sudden.'

The Judge sniggered at the feeble mortal. He took the man's face between his palms and blew against it, cold and crisp.

'Can you feel that?' the man shuddered, turning to the group who were shaking their heads in dismissal. They were reaching into bags for snacks – pulling open crisp packets and pork scratchings, nibbling on chocolate bars and swigging beer from cans or bottles they'd brought with them.

Suddenly curious, The Judge stepped forward into the man. Literally. To his surprise, the Judge found that, rather than passing through the man, he was surrounded in a warm cocoon of human flesh. He stretched out his essence in its new environment, sending an icy wave of shock and fear through his human host.

The man crumpled to the floor, cross-legged. He felt faint and completely out-of-sorts.

'Jeremy?' asked the woman with red hair and grey roots. 'You all right?'

'I feel…weird,' he confessed, his skin turning a sickly green colour.

The Judge, nestled in the man's core, had never felt so powerful in death. Sapping and guzzling and swallowing the man's energy into his own transparent self, Jeffreys used it all to force the man's hands to lift the whisky to his awaiting lips.

'I don't think whisky will help matters…' the woman interjected, to sounds of agreement from their friends.

The Judge let out a rasp of satisfaction as the burning whisky slid down the man's throat and filled his belly with fire.

'Shut your mouth,' he spat.

The group stared at him, aghast.

'Jeremy!' cried one, taking the bottle from him. 'How much of this have you had?'

'Not enough,' he barked.

Inside Jeremy, the Judge chuckled. Oh, this was magical. He could feel the man's body rejecting his spirit, attacking him, trying to flush him out.

'I'm going to be sick,' Jeremy said suddenly, clamping a hand over his mouth as he got up and ran for the bathroom.

And in his place, unbeknownst to the guests, sat the Judge, rolling with laughter that sent the thieves in the walls quivering.

Fifteen

Emlyn was starting to get used to comprehensive school. Sort of. After numerous wrong turns down shoe-scuffed corridors and a few marks for tardiness in the class register, he had managed to get to grips with the layout of the building. The library had even opened its marvellous doors at last – giving him a place to relax and enjoy break periods somewhere that wasn't a fluorescent-lit corridor.

The librarian was a quiet, weedy man with nostrils that flared so large it was rumoured he could vacuum the floor with his nose (should he want to, for some strange reason.) Emlyn thought it was a bit mean of students to say so, but choked back a smile when the librarian carefully stamped his books and handed them over, hairy nostrils flared as he nodded goodbye.

In truth, Emlyn didn't need to take books from the library; his mam and dad kept him well stocked, and most of the books on his shelves had been read two or three times. But there was something about the library's packed shelves, and the way that the new-book smell from the Recent Releases shelf mingled with the book-dust scent of older things that made him want more. He could pick up a brand-new paperback and perhaps be the very first person to ever leaf through its crisp, white pages. Or he could find something older, buried on a shelf in the back, dog-eared edges whispering the history of its previous readers. What secrets were tucked away in those books, just waiting for someone to find? Soon Emlyn's rucksack bulged with the added bulk of all the books he'd devour, as soon as he found a spare moment.

School life was settling, and Emlyn felt a sense of relief. But of course, it couldn't last. One afternoon, on his way back to registration class, he noticed too late that he was about to pass the three boys who had hounded him that day in the bathroom.

Emlyn had been idling along, thinking about getting his mark and how heavy his rucksack felt, when someone had loudly announced that his shoe laces were untied.

He looked down, baffled, and in that split second, a hand came up from beneath him and slapped his cheek with a sharp sting.

The students lining the corridor were all roughly two years above Emlyn. He'd also learned from listening in on other students that his tormentors' names were Carwyn, Ryan and Lee. Three lads who prodded, teased and bullied the majority of the comprehensive school population. So, Emlyn was pretty quick to avoid their little gang, unless he let his guard down.

'He hasn't even got laces on his shoes and he still looked down!' mocked Carwyn, clutching a belly full of fizzy cola and Walkers salted crisps.

'You seem distracted. Were you thinking up ghost stories you can use to rip people off?' asked Ryan with a bitter bite.

Emlyn dodged another incoming slap and rushed down the corridor, away from the jeers and laughter, insults and accusations. His heart pounded and his cheeks bloomed red, but he felt somewhat comforted when a PE teacher – a Scotsman called Mr McInnes – saw Emlyn's distressed expression and gave a headshake of disapproval in the evil trio's direction.

Not that a headshake of disapproval was likely to stop the boys from doing it all again in future…

*   *   *

The most diabolical act from the wicked trio came on a day when Emlyn's mam had been unable to give him a lift home from school. She had been unwell and unfit to drive and after dropping him off at the gates with a hacking cough and a fistful of damp tissue.

Forced to face a school bus when the final lesson (Maths. Yawn.) was complete, Emlyn hung back from the crowd. The other kids shuffled onto an old, awaiting school bus, its weathered windows murky with rain and dirt. He tried to appear at ease, as if he caught the school bus home regularly. But it wasn't long before –

'Well if it isn't Mr Creepy!' Ryan yelled over the sounds of chattering kids, all glad to be going home for the day. Many were staring down at mobile phone screens, distracted by social media pages and photos to scroll through. They weren't paying Emlyn any attention. 'The school bus is finally good enough for him!'

Emlyn had retreated to a seat by a window, trying his hardest to focus on the world beyond its dirty glass. The rain had started to pick up, dotting the road with darker splodges, and crows were getting into a frenzy on a pylon line, flapping fitfully and taking to the sky in search of better shelter.

Carwyn, Ryan and Lee nudged a boy out of the seat next to Emlyn – situated halfway down the bus – and made sure he was surrounded.

'No teachers here now, Mr Creepy,' Lee pointed out, falsely jovial.

Emlyn's face grew hot with panic as the boys loomed closer, and he flinched away as Ryan, in the seat behind his own, reached over and flicked his ear with a deep chuckle. It stung. Much like the time a bee had stung Emlyn's knee when he'd been kneeling in the grass. He hadn't realised the bee was beneath him and as he watched his skin swell where the sting had penetrated, the bee buzzed and slowly died nearby.

'How come you barely talk?' Carwyn asked, shoulder to shoulder with Emlyn, as if they were close companions. He reached down for the rucksack between Emlyn's legs. 'Don't,' Emlyn warned, snapping his hands out to clutch his belongings.

'Why? You have spell books in here or something?'

'Don't be absurd,' Emlyn replied, finding a mite of bravery in his guts. 'I only live next to an *allegedly* haunted house. I'm not a witch. I don't dress all in black. I don't talk with spirits. I don't do much of anything. I'm normal, okay? So leave off.'

Carwyn wrestled the bag from Emlyn regardless of his protest.

'What are you doing?' Emlyn shrieked as they played an unevenly matched game of tug of war.

'Give it,' Carwyn growled back.

Lee slipped a hand over the seat's headrest behind Carwyn and started yanking the bag with him. All the while Ryan egged them on. When Carwyn, with a mighty heave, had the bag at last, he swivelled in his seat, presenting a flustered Emlyn with a view of his back. Kids around them were staring, heads turned away from glowing mobile screens, though no one moved to help.

Carwyn pulled the bag open and fished around with a fumbling paw, noticing a half-drunk bottle of water. He loosened the lid and dropped the bottle back in with a grin before snatching up a thick, unlabelled book. It's soft leather cover drew his fingers.

'This isn't a school exercise book. So, what have we got here then? A diary?' Emlyn thumped Carwyn's arm and tried to stand up, but Lee and Ryan pinned him into his seat.

'Ooh. It's poetry and stories! How cute.' He cleared his throat and the bus seemed to quieten – even the blustering, croaking engine died down. Carwyn picked out a few lines of Emlyn's neat handwriting and read the section aloud:

'The tree grew strong and mighty
And thick white branches spread

With books that dangled high above
Their pages crisp, unread

I plucked one down from the foliage
The people held their tongues
I read aloud a story;
Enchanting parents, daughters, sons'

'Mr Creepy's a poet and he knows it, boys,' Lee cried, ruffling Emlyn's hair with a heavy hand.

Carwyn was laughing at his own performance, re-reading the lines in what he deemed to be a posh English accent.

Emlyn wriggled out from beneath his captor and made a grab for the book. Then he gaped in horror as Carwyn budged two girls out of the seats across the aisle and pried open the small, slanted window there. He held Emlyn's book perilously close to its open jaws...

'No! Don't!' Emlyn screamed.

Carwyn's eyes flashed. He liked the tone of distress in the boy's voice. Carwyn was in charge of this moment. The one in control of the suffering. The sadness. The pain.

'What good are baby stories, Creepy? This is the real world. Start living in it.'

He slid the notebook through the gap in the window like a package through a letterbox and, with a taunting waggle of his eyebrows, let the leather-bound collection of Emlyn's work-in-progress tumble out into the autumn wind. It quickly disappeared.

Sixteen

With the notebook gone, the bullies dispersed with sniggers, leaving Emlyn to mourn its loss. No one bothered to fill the empty seat at his side, perhaps afraid that Emlyn's bad luck would rub off on them too.

When the bus came to a screeching halt at Emlyn's stop, he hopped out onto the roadside with his head down against the spitting rain and shuffled up the lane to his house, avoiding the eyes of a young couple standing outside the inn, their lit cigarettes vomiting smoke into the country air.

Inside the house, he checked that his mam was distracted elsewhere (she was in bed breathing noisily through a blocked nose, eyes closed against a headache) and then rushed to the back door where he entered the ghastly, unkempt garden (every summer his dad planned on clearing it. Every summer, he found something more pressing to do elsewhere). There, under a faded, moss-green ceramic frog, was a set of spare shed keys. The damp smell inside the shed wrinkled Emlyn's nose, and he kept a wary eye out for cobwebs. At the back, he found what he was looking for: his old bike, leaning against the wall and tangled in garden hose.

When he finally managed to wrestle the bike outside, Emlyn sighed in relief. The tyres, luckily, still had air in them. He hadn't ridden a bike in a while. The days of childhood races down country lanes were long over. His cousin – the slightly older and longer-legged Rhiannon – had always beat him anyway, which he'd hated because she was a girl, borrowing his mam's bike. Technically, a girl's bike shouldn't be able to beat a BMX, no matter how long your legs were!

Emlyn swung his legs over the seat and was about to take off when a niggle in his brain reminded him of something essential he was forgetting. His mam would clip him across the ear if she knew he was out riding without a helmet, even if it did make him look like a dork.

Begrudgingly, he ducked back into the shed and found his blue helmet with the flaking Power Rangers sticker on its top (that's how long it had been since he'd worn it). If he wasn't in such a darn rush, he would have picked the sticker off. But all he had time for was the removal of a spindly spider that had found its home inside.

Now, Emlyn rode with the same fury he'd had during those summer races, only there was no cousin to compete with and no warm summer sun on his back. The cold bit his knuckles as he retraced the route the school bus had taken, praying no cars were lurking around the corners of those narrow country lanes. Luckily for him, all was quiet, and when the meandering lanes were behind him and the cars started to become more frequent, he slowed just a little to be on the safe side. All the while, he kept a sharp eye out for his notebook.

But infuriatingly, it was as the comprehensive school filled his line of vision that Emlyn accepted his notebook was lost. Well and truly gone for good. All his ideas and stories. All his hard work. His little piece of what made him feel real: a physical memento of his imagination.

Emlyn seethed.

He wanted to thump Carwyn.

His knuckles turned white as he gripped the handlebars of his bike, trekking back the way he'd come, feeling his clothes dampen with sweat and his body straining with effort. 'Emlyn!' called his dad, as he was pushing the bike around the back of the house. He was putting a clinking bag from the inn into a black wheelie-bin. 'Where did you go? You shot off and didn't even stop to say you were back!'

Emlyn couldn't tell if his dad was angry or not. He conjured a lie. 'I saw something weird on the bus ride home. Thought it was an animal, still alive, but hurt. A fox. Or small dog. I dunno.'

'Did you find it?'

'No. Whatever it was, it's gone,' he said, leading the bike through the back gate to avoid further questioning.

'Well, next time, at least tell one of us you're home from school first.'

'Sorry, Dad!' he yelled over his shoulder.

With the bike and helmet stashed away, the shed locked and its key returned to its hiding place, Emlyn slunk into his bedroom, buzzing with the adrenaline of white-hot anger laced with woe. His eyes were suddenly drawn to the school rucksack against his wardrobe where he'd tossed it. On the floor surrounding it, there shimmered a clear puddle. He tugged the rucksack's zipper and immediately saw the plastic water bottle that he'd forgotten: the one Carwyn had opened and allowed to fall amidst Emlyn's belongings.

All the library books and school notebooks were sopping wet, crumpled – in some cases even unreadable, thanks to the non-waterproof handwriting pen he favoured in class.

He put his hand to his face and let the bag slip to the floor with a thunk.

He'd been strong up until then.

But thinking about the boys surrounding him, tugging his bag and notebook away, making him feel so small and powerless… they'd destroyed his belongings with zero remorse.

He'd have to replace the school workbooks, of course. And pay for the library books, probably. And his own leather-bound collection…

Emlyn's emotions got the better of him at last.

He dived onto his bed and wept.

* * *

Emlyn's bedroom door creaked open with a subtle tapping on wood. His mam peered through the gap and found him in bed, lying on his side in the dark. He had a book open and face down beside him. But his eyes were closed – his cheek nestled in the open palm of one hand.

'You okay, boyo?' She pushed the door an inch more. He gave her a nod, followed by silence. 'Your dad has a dinner for you at the inn. I just haven't been up to facing the kitchen today, I'm sorry.'

'It's fine. I'll grab it after,' he said stiffly.

She narrowed her eyes and pushed the door as far as it would go, letting the landing light flood the darkness of his bedroom. 'You are feeling all right?'

Emlyn shook his head. No. No, he really wasn't.

She touched a hand to his forehead. 'There's no temperature. Perhaps it's just your body adapting to the changes? New school. New environment. New people. Early mornings again –'

'Yeah, maybe,' he muttered, closing his eyes.

'You might feel better if you eat something?' She took a tissue from her pocket and wiped her snuffly nose. 'It's lasagne.'

Emlyn's favourite.

'I just have a headache, Mam. Waiting for it to go.'

'Well, all right then. I'm here if you need me.'

He spread his lips in a thin, appreciative smile and his mam lifted the book to study its cover. '*Skellig*. David Almond. That's a good one.' She tapped the paperback and then frowned. 'Why's it damp?'

Emlyn's eyes widened. His mam looked at the radiator automatically, as if she had some sort of radar for these kinds of tragedies. More of his books – mainly library stock – were hanging awkwardly against the warm metal.

'It was an accident. My water bottle at school.'

She sighed and put *Skellig* back on the bed, face down as it had been. 'You need to be more careful.'

'I know. I know… I'm sorry.' His eyes were stinging with shame for the damage. He didn't want her to think he didn't care about his books. He loved them. More than anything.

They were his gateways to new lives and new worlds. He could be anything in a book. Anyone.

'Rest your eyes for five. I'll bring you hot chocolate,' she said, kissing him atop his scraggly head of dark hair.

But when she came back upstairs with his brimming mug, Emlyn was fast asleep.

Seventeen

Emlyn awoke in the middle of the night. He'd been dreaming that he was in the kitchen, opening one cupboard after another, looking for something to eat. But the cupboards were empty, except for a single carton of salt. He flipped the lid with a pop and let the granules dance and skitter over the palm of his hand. He wet his index finger with his tongue and started eating the salt, which only increased his thirst and hunger until it became painful.

In reality, his mouth had a sour taste and his throat felt prickly with pain. Emlyn's empty stomach gurgled, and he rubbed his dry eyes until they were clear enough to see the time on his robot clock: 2 a.m. A cold mug of hot chocolate with a creamy, unappetising film on its surface sat on his bedside table. He vaguely remembered his mam offering to bring it to him earlier that night.

He rolled onto his side and bunched up his pillows, forcing his mind to settle into sleep again. But his skull started to throb, harder and faster.

He touched his forehead with a palm and felt moisture.

Groaning, he rolled again, on to his stomach with his face turned to the bedside table.

Sleep pulled him under again, though not gently. He tossed and turned, eyes rolling about beneath his lids as he dreamed in slushy, ragged images. In his dream he saw the Judge slamming down his gavel and pointing his finger at... Emlyn. Emlyn was surrounded by people he didn't recognise, wearing the mucky clothes of farmers and townsfolk from some era not his own. Some of his audience were gawping at him, eyes ablaze with concern. Others were red-cheeked and stern-faced, bellowing words to their companions, which Emlyn couldn't make out.

What Emlyn could ascertain from his situation was this: he was inside the Skirrid Inn. It looked like Rooms One and Two, only with no wall partitioning them – the old court room, it must be. It was cold, and packed full of bodies eager for entertainment.

'Fetch the rope,' the Judge commanded.

Emlyn turned to see two men approach, a hangman's noose between them.

'NO!' he screamed.

Another voice echoed his cry. A girl's voice.

'NO!' she protested. 'Don't harm the boy!'

The crowd silenced and let her through. She was tall, and older than Emlyn, her face pale and glistening like fresh snow. Stray strands of dark hair, escaped from the bun on top of her head, whipped around her pointed chin as she pushed hurriedly through the crowd

'He brought me back from the Grey Place!' the girl cried. 'I need him!'

The noose was wriggled over his head and Emlyn felt the pressure of hands dragging him backwards to the stairwell outside the door. They really were going to hang him.

'I NEED HIM!' the woman cried out, reaching for his hand as he passed.

'Emlyn!'

Emlyn bolted upright and choked on his own surprise at finding his mam looming over his bed. One hand gripped his arm, which he'd been using to push the duvet from his flailing body. His mam was messy-haired and wearing her dressing gown inside out – the tag was showing near her hip.

'You gave me one heck of a heart attack!' she said breathlessly. 'I could hear you calling out in your sleep. I thought someone had broken into the house!'

Emlyn lifted himself upright, just as his dad emerged from the shadows.

'Everything okay?' he asked, knobbly knees catching the light from the landing.

'I'm fine,' Emlyn sighed, his throat burning. 'Nightmares. I feel really gross. Achy and –'

His mam put a hand to his forehead.

'You're boiling, love. Grab him a glass of water, would you?' she shot over her shoulder.

Emlyn's dad disappeared.

'I think you'd better stay home with me tomorrow. You need sleep. Fluids. And to get some food in you. Probably caught what I've had…'

Emlyn said nothing, but accepted the glass of tap water on his dad's return.

'I'll call the secretary at the school and let them know in the morning.'

She started to make for the door, Emlyn's dad following.

'Come get us if you need anything. Your dad can go out and fetch some more Lemsip when the shops are open. I've downed the whole box, I'm afraid. The cupboards are pretty bare. There's paracetamol, if you want some?' she said in an apologetic tone. 'Put your audio book on if you can't sleep. It might help you drift off.'

Emlyn smiled weakly as his parents left, the light in the hallway switching to blackness.

Staying home from school was the best suggestion he'd heard all week. He could relax at last. Forget about Carwyn, Lee and Ryan at every turn of the corridor. Forget about the ringing of his alarm clock in his ears when he most wanted to close his eyes. And he could try to forget the sound of that gavel striking wood; the Judge's face creased menacingly from above; the cries of a woman, whom Emlyn felt a sickening sense he'd heard before…

Eighteen

As the headache worsened and his nose grew stuffy and drippy at the nostrils, Emlyn spent most of the time feeling sorry for himself. Sickness often felt like a bad dream to him. He dipped in and out of sleep, not knowing where he was, or what day he'd landed in. He tossed and turned and wiped his nose until the skin cracked around the nostrils. His throat felt thick with mucus and all food tasted bland and unappetising.

He was allowed more than one day off school to recover – and he was extremely grateful to his mam for it – but on the third day, the aches eased and he found himself able to read his book without slipping into a fever dream.

His mam, on the other hand, had fully recovered. On the Friday, early evening time, she asked Emlyn to join her at the Skirrid to wash dinner dishes, whilst Denise had her half an hour break. Emlyn had confessed to feeling a lot better at this point, but didn't like the idea of entering the inn for any reason whatsoever. In fact, if he never set foot in there again, he'd die happy.

But how could he say no after days of her waiting on him hand and foot? She'd brought him both hot and cold drinks as he'd wished, made him fresh soups, and brought him chicken nuggets with ketchups when he was feeling a bit stronger. She'd even given up a few boxes of her expensive tissues, the ones with aloe and moisturiser in, to soothe his raw nose.

Reluctantly he joined her at the busy inn, taking deep breaths to stave off the rise of hyperventilation. And what he didn't expect – as his hands softened in the warm bubbly water of the kitchen sink as he worked – was news of visitors asking for him.

'Emlyn! There are some lads out here for you. Friends from school?'

He dropped a plate into the bowl. It cracked against another. Cursing, he picked up the two halves and quickly stuffed them in the bin. His mam hated to see broken items. Everything at the inn had history; a story. To break it was not only bad luck, but the end of something special. Or at least that's how she put it.

Friends from school?

Surely it wasn't who he thought it could be. They wouldn't have the confidence. They wouldn't take the risk… would they?

He dried his hands in a towel and left the kitchen apprehensively, forgetting he was still in the pinny his parents insisted he wear when cleaning, with the Ghostbusters' slogan 'I ain't afraid of no ghost' on the front pocket. ('The punters will love it,' his dad had insisted, when he'd brought them home from a pop-up market in town).

Emlyn's skin prickled as he entered the main bar to see the three faces he'd dreaded the most.

'All right there, Em?' said Carwyn, with a smile like that of a wolf dressed as a grandma, intent on fooling Red Riding Hood. Lee and Ryan wore matching grins. 'We thought we'd swing by and see how you were. And your mam here said we could look around upstairs too.'

Emlyn darted a look at his mam. She was busy with a customer ordering a meal from the main menu hanging on the wall.

'Let's see what all the fuss is about then,' Carwyn urged.

Emlyn gritted his teeth. 'No.'

'No? What kind of a place is this where you turn customers away?'

'You aren't a customer,' Emlyn bit back. 'Just go.'

Carwyn took a step forward, his chest and forehead mere inches from Emlyn's. 'Either you go get the keys and open the rooms for us to have a look around, or we make a scene right here, right now –'

'We've got guests going upstairs soon –' Emlyn tried.

'We won't be long. And your mam said it was fine with her.'

As if on cue, Emlyn's mam plonked three keys on the bar top. 'There you go, love. Show your friends around, but don't take too long. The guests will be finishing their meals in the dining room any minute.'

Emlyn's mouth opened, but the words wouldn't form. What could he say?

Ryan scooped the keys off the top as Carwyn winked. 'Lead the way.'

With each step, Emlyn felt guarded and poised for an attack. The boys were keen on his heels, clonking up the wooden steps and snickering about something. Emlyn vaguely wondered if they'd stuck some sort of offensive note on his back to be causing them so much amusement. But during a feigned scratch of his spine, he couldn't feel anything attached.

'It's smaller than I thought,' Lee commented.

'The corridor seems small. The rooms are large,' Emlyn retorted. He fumbled with the key in the lock. 'There. Room One. Go have a look.' Emlyn planned on standing outside and waiting, but then imagined the boys taking or breaking something. Reluctantly, he followed behind them.

Carwyn stuck his nose up. 'Just seems like a normal room to me.'

Emlyn frowned.

'Tell us about the ghosts then,' Ryan prompted.

'No. You're not a paying customer. You're just here to be nosy.'

The boys glared at each other with malicious smirks. They couldn't deny it.

The group of wayward lads proceeded to Room Two. It was colder, but only because one of the windows had been left open. Emlyn's dad had done a quick window cleaning session after the last guests had departed.

'People pay good money for this?' Carwyn scoffed, poking the duvet on the four-poster bed.

Emlyn ignored his jibe. They moved on to the third and final guest room, and as Emlyn pushed the door open –

'What the hell?!'

He jumped backwards, barging into the lads behind him.

'Easy, tiger,' Carwyn grumbled, gripping Emlyn's shoulders to steady him. 'That trick won't work on us. We don't scare easily.'

Emlyn gaped ahead, his eyes wide. He didn't even care that Carwyn had a firm hand on his shoulder.

He was speechless. Frozen. Entranced.

The boys thought Emlyn was entertaining them – trying to make their stone-cold hearts jolt in fear of the unknown. But Emlyn was truly seeing the unthinkable. His mind felt as if it were rocketing through space, buffeting against stars and galaxies. His stomach churned, acids bubbling, and his heart pounded so hard he thought he might die from it.

There was a woman asleep on the bed, her dark hair fanned out against the pillow.

And she simply couldn't be a guest. Right? *No.* Yes? Maybe? Ahh! *What was this?* His mam would have told him if there was someone already upstairs. Not to mention – there was a soft, faint light glowing from the centre of her chest, near where her heart would have been.

Carwyn and his cronies moved around the rigid Emlyn, inspecting the small space as if the woman wasn't lying there, her bare feet peeking from beneath her long brown skirts. They didn't seem to care one jot that she could wake any moment to four young boys standing over her, three of which were mooching about invasively.

Emlyn's skin went hot. His chest flared with

116

what felt like striking lightning. He was fearful and amazed all at once.

There's a

woman

on the bed –

The words repeated loudly in his head, in time with his racing heart.

'What?' Carwyn demanded, when he noticed Emlyn had been as pale as milk and silent as stone. The bully knocked over a picture frame with a clatter – clearly something he'd been itching to do since they'd started their tour.

'We need to leave,' Emlyn croaked at last.

The woman on the bed peeled open her eyes slowly at the sound of his voice and turned her head in his direction. Her long, mousy brown hair gathered into a tail between her shoulder blades as she lifted herself into a seated position. Her eyes locked onto Emlyn's. It seared him from the inside.

They stared for three long seconds.

'You can see me?' she whispered.

Emlyn dropped the handful of keys with a clunk.

'We have to go,' he barked, with as much authority as he could muster. 'NOW.'

The boys curled their lips in disapproval and in turn, they hissed and growled and snarled in Emlyn's face on passing. They clomped with unnecessary force down the stairs to the main bar, murmuring about how 'rubbish' the place was and that it was all just a 'joke.'

'Don't go!' the woman on the bed called out, reaching for Emlyn as he backed away.

He didn't even bother to lock the door behind him.

He just ran.

Nineteen

The three bullies left with ominous promises of 'see you in school Monday,' waving and smiling warmly in what Emlyn felt was a disgusting performance for his mam. She smiled back with a glow about her – as if she were proud to see her son with 'friends.' How sad she would be if she knew the real reason they had visited.

'You have the keys for me?' she asked.

'What?' Emlyn replied in a sharp, jittery tone. His head swam with images of the woman on the bed.

A… a dead woman. And her face! Wasn't she the same woman he'd… well… dreamt of recently? She looked so familiar–

'The room keys?' His mam waggled her waiting fingers.

'Oh.' He cast his eyes to the ceiling. His skin ran hot and cold simultaneously.

'Seriously, Emlyn? You left them upstairs?'

'I got… There was...' he stumbled.

She scowled.

'There was something up there!' he blurted, unexpectedly.

Her brows slowly lifted from their jagged, unamused position to something more like disbelief. 'So, you're saying you dropped the keys because you saw an apparition?'

Emlyn scratched the back of his neck, checking nervously over his shoulder that no one was listening. In a building where people championed experiences with ghosts, he was still certain he sounded absurd at the mere mention of 'seeing' anything.

'Well…' He choked on his words.

'Emlyn, this is all very fascinating.' His mam took him by the shoulders. 'And I can't wait to hear all the details, but right now, boyo, I need you to go grab me those keys. I can't leave the bar.'

Someone was tapping a glass as she spoke. She registered the noise with a flicker of acknowledgment in their direction.

'They can't hurt you,' she implored, moving away from her son.

'Mam –'

'It was probably one of your friends anyway!'

It was Emlyn's turn to scowl. 'I don't think so somehow.'

He bit his lip. Flexed his fingers and clenched his fists. Swallowed hard. Forced his legs to move.

Returning to Room Three was the last thing he wanted right now. Dealing with dead people was never something he'd signed up for! He was a kid. He should be in bed playing video games and texting friends about lame teachers. If he had friends, that is. Then again, what if he had just made one of the biggest unexplainable discoveries of his town? Maybe even the country? Or the world?

He stopped and sidled up to the bar, nodding to the man with his pint. In a careful aside, he asked, 'What protection is there against ghosts? I mean, is there something you and Dad do when you see weird things?'

'Emlyn.' His mam huffed fiercely. 'I don't have

time for this. The guests are waiting to get upstairs. Now, boyo.'

'Okay! Okay! I'll go.'

His body wanted to abort. His legs felt jelly-like. But with each accomplished step upwards, his curiosity was beginning to pique. He was like Alice in Wonderland, discovering new and crazy things the further he went into unknown territory. Giant caterpillars. Smiling cats that could turn invisible. Queens with a passion for beheading –

Gulp.

Okay, maybe that wasn't the most comforting of thoughts.

There's a young woman on the bed in Room Three, he calmly reminded himself. *Just a pale, sleepy, glowy woman.*

He took a deep breath outside the door. Nudged it open.

'H... Hello?' he said, as quiet as a magpie ruffling feathers in the rain. He swallowed as he peered into the room.

The young woman was still there – sat on the edge of the bed, with long skirts rumpled and kissing her exposed ankles. Her face sparkled with unnatural energy, and there was a glow at the centre of her chest twinkling yellow like a lone star.

Emlyn inched inside and stood as far from the bed as he could.

'You see me?' the woman asked carefully.

Emlyn gulped as her words trickled like cold water into his ears. Her voice sounded tinny. It reminded him of a time in primary school, when the teacher had attached string to two cans and showed students you could speak to each other from across the room when talking into their round openings.

This woman was clearly not of this earth and yet Emlyn could see her before him, watching him as he watched back.

'I… I see you,' he managed.

They remained frozen in bewilderment, until Emlyn remembered his mam was waiting downstairs and probably getting antsy. He snatched up the keys on the floor and tucked them in a pocket, all the while keeping the woman in his sights.

'Are you leaving again?' she asked, panicked. 'Stay with me? For a while? I didn't think I was capable of talking to the living. Perhaps… you can help me?'

Emlyn had his hand on the door handle. Adrenaline made his heart loud.

'I'll… come back,' he said, hesitantly. 'I'll come back. Tomorrow. Afternoon. When the guests are gone and the rooms have been cleaned. Will you be here then?'

She lowered her gaze to the floor sadly. 'I can't be sure. But I should think so. Yes.'

'Well,' Emlyn replied. 'I'll come over. Just in case, I guess.'

She nodded. 'I'm grateful. You have no idea how much so!'

He could tell from her tone of voice that she meant it. And now that she was sat so clearly before him, he could also tell she was most certainly the woman he had dreamt of.

The one who had asked for his help.

'Is your name Fanny?'

She looked surprised. 'How do you know that?'

'It's a long story,' he explained, none too helpfully. He readied himself to take his leave. 'Tomorrow. We'll... talk.'

*   *   *

Emlyn slapped cold water into his face at the bathroom sink the following morning, having dipped in and out of a weird dream all night. He'd dreamt that the ghost-woman had been standing in his school registration room, but no one else could see her. She'd followed him everywhere. Around the school yard. Down corridors. Into the library. Always staring. Never speaking.

But it didn't stop Emlyn from wanting to see her – Fanny – the next day. A promise was a promise, right? If he said he was going to do something, he would. Even if that promise involved talking to the dead in a creepy room.

The cold water from the tap eased the blurriness of Emlyn's sleep-deprived brain. Moving mechanically, like a wind-up toy, he put on his clothes faster than ever before – though his socks were not quite the correct pairing. (He left them as they were, too rushed to change them.)

When it was safe to slip over, Emlyn said nothing of his intentions at the inn whilst he lifted the key to room three from its hook. His bedraggled dad was busy taking lunch orders and his mam was doing some 'much needed spring cleaning' back at the main house, now that she had well and truly shaken her sickness bug.

Maintaining a stealthy pace (so as not to arouse suspicion), Emlyn made his way upstairs, where he clicked and clonked the key into its home and pushed open the door.

'Fanny?' His voice wavered. The adrenaline was

almost unbearable this time. He understood now, why people collapsed at music concerts because of their overwhelming excitement.

Quiet.

'Fanny?'

He was about to call for a third time, when hands stemmed from beneath the wooden bed frame; two icy branches with long, bony fingers. They clawed at the floor as a face emerged, with wide dark eyes that reflected Emlyn's figure. Fanny stood – a whole head taller than him – and patted down her skirts.

'You were true to your word.' She sounded pleased. Surprised, even.

'Y… Yes. I came as soon as I could. Sorry if you had to wait–'

'It's all right. It's just… nice. That you see all of me. You can, right?'

He nodded like a clown sprung from a jack-in-the-box. 'It's like you're glowing. Like a night light.'

'Am I?' She looked down at herself. Stretched her arms before her and admired her hands.

'It's in your centre,' Emlyn gestured to his chest. 'In here.'

She placed a hand over the area her heart had once been. 'How peculiar. But then again… I'm…' She broke off.

'Dead?'

Sadness infiltrated her expression.

'I think I've been dreaming about you,' Emlyn confessed. 'You were calling to me. The first time. You mentioned something called the Grey Place. Does that ring any bells to you?'

Fanny suddenly looked at the servant's bell on the table. It was a turn of phrase she probably wasn't used to and had failed to understand.

'I heard the bell, yes.' She wandered to the table full of trinkets and touched the bell's handle. 'I came from the Grey Place. When someone called me…'

'You mean, you weren't here? Before?' Emlyn moved to her side, sensing the cold coming from her in waves. He picked up the bell and turned it over in his hands, checking for any special qualities he might not have noticed when he'd first handled it.

'The Grey Place is a between. At least, I think it is. The bell brought me back.'

Emlyn's eyes sparkled with realisation. 'I think it was me.'

'What?'

'I rang the bell. I brought it here the other day. My mam sent me up with it. I rang it a few times, actually.'

'Then… maybe that's why only you can see me?'

They looked at the bell in his hand and then lifted their chins to face one another.

'I'm sorry,' Emlyn said, in a small remorseful voice. 'If I'd known…'

She shook her head, sending her hair fluttering about her shoulders. 'There's no blame here. I can see you're sincere and honest.'

'Guests, in the past, said they heard the bell ringing. But we never had a real bell here. So how? It doesn't make sense.'

'Echoes,' Fanny said, simply. 'The walls talk sometimes. They hold memory just as much as life does. Or… maybe my employer was here looking for me? He used to keep a bell in his pocket, you see.'

'I feel so terrible.' Emlyn put the bell back on its doily, believing he'd caused enough damage by holding it already. He certainly didn't want to lure more of the dead from their sleep. 'Were you at peace? Before the bell called you?'

Fanny sighed thoughtfully. 'I was nothing at all. I just existed. There was no memory. No real feeling. Just waiting. Waiting in emptiness.'

'Oh. So… this is better? Being here?'

Her gaze flitted to the wall that separated her room from the old court.

'No.'

She slunk on to the bed and drew her knees up to her chest. Emlyn – feeling weirdly like he was intruding on a woman that wasn't even meant to exist – sat timidly beside her, his shoulder very nearly touching her icy essence. He didn't know what he could say to console a ghost. He faltered for a moment, then at last he said, 'I can't believe I'm sat here, talking with you.'

She sniffed. 'It is a marvel.'

'Do you think there's a reason?'

'A reason for what?'

'This. Talking. Communicating. The dreams. All of it. There's always a reason, right? This can't be for nothing.'

Emlyn was thinking excitedly about his books. The harrowing journeys, the good-versus-evil, the challenges. The happy endings. Was this his purpose? Was this his adventure?

'There's got to be something I can do. To help you.'

Fanny wiped ghostly tendrils of hair from her eyes and turned to face the boy. 'I just want to find my sister,' she said, with a hint of sorrow. 'I want to know what happened to her. If I have to stay here forever and be tormented by that horrid, vile beast of a man –'

Emlyn was awed for a moment. 'You're talking

about Jeffreys, aren't you? The Judge? He's here too, isn't he?'

Fanny suddenly looked nervous.

'If I were to advise you on anything this day, boy, it would be to not utter his name, lest you wake him. He's not a lover of the living.'

Her warning sent a shard of ice into Emlyn's innards. Fanny was quite a placid spirit, it seemed. The Judge probably wasn't quite so tolerant of intruders with questions.

'Why don't you go? Run away?' he asked.

'I can't. I physically can't. I'm rooted here. If I could run, I would. Believe me.'

'Tell me all about him, then. The Judge.' He chose his words carefully. 'Maybe we can figure something out together?' Emlyn encouraged.

She thought on it briefly.

'Not in here.'

She glided across the room and soundlessly walked through the wall leading to the adjoining bathroom. Emlyn found her nestled in the bathtub with her legs crossed – a bizarre sight indeed.

'Run the water,' she instructed, gesturing to the shower knob. 'The living are like vermin to him. He will stay away if he thinks you're in here washing.'

Emlyn turned the knob and allowed the water

to skitter scatter into the tub, where his new and unusual friend sat perfectly dry, even though she was exposed to the stream. He perched on the rim of the toilet seat and craned his neck to listen to her softly spoken words.

In the confined space, Fanny began telling her story.

Twenty

Judge Jeffreys carefully placed an ear in the vicinity of the bathroom door. He had no substance to physically press skin to wood, but he mimicked the action to focus on the voices the other side.

What an interesting twist in the tale, he thought to himself bitterly. The maiden has found herself a knight! And a way to communicate with a human child – and lo, she's decided to use this talent to speak ill of me!

He quietly seethed, gnashing his teeth. When suddenly, a voice over his shoulder made for an interesting new twist...

*   *   *

'Emlyn! Are you up there?'

Emlyn sprang from the toilet seat. He checked his watch. Hours had gone by. Hours of talking to Fanny about the Judge and about her life – serving a family who had lived at the inn before she had died of a sickness that had taken her unexpectedly. She had sent word to her sister, but no one had come to her aid or to say goodbye, and it became blatantly apparent to Emlyn that this was a strong contender as to why Fanny was here, full of fear in the afterlife.

What had happened to the young and pregnant Emily Price?

Emlyn had allowed the shower to run and run and run – wasting water, though he'd had the good sense to let it run cold instead of hot. He'd told Fanny a little of himself as well. His childhood. His passion for books. His general woes with the new and scary comprehensive school. In comparison to Fanny, his existence sounded cushioned and fluffy, up until the bullying episodes.

Their talking had also solved the mystery of the sobs and shrieks he'd been hearing – puzzle pieces, at last, falling in to place.

'EMLYN?'

'Coming!' he yelled with his hands cupped into the shape of a megaphone.

Fanny stood, her skirts trailing in the water that raced towards the plughole. Not a single drop of liquid stained her outfit.

'Will I see you again?' she asked, with a desperate curiosity. 'You'll come back?'

'Of course,' he assured her. 'I want to help figure this out. You're not meant to be here. You're good and kind. Surely you were called from the Grey Place for a reason.'

'You're very sweet, boy,' she said, though twisting her fingers nervously.

'I don't want Jeffreys to hurt you,' Emlyn said softly.

I can be a hero, he thought. *I can do this.* What could the ghost of a long-dead judge do to him, after all? If he was going to hurt Emlyn, he would have done it by now. All those evenings he'd spent on the cobwebbed sofa, writing his stories. All the times he'd been upstairs alone, stripping the beds of their dirty sheets for his mam. He'd never felt so much as a breath against his neck –

'EMLYN!' came another yell from downstairs. The urgency was definite.

'Look, I've really got to go. When I get a chance, I'll come back. I'm going to do some research. See what I can find.'

Fanny nodded. 'I hope it's a fruitful venture.'

'Goodbye!' Emlyn said, halfway out the door, just as he ran face first into –

'Dad!'

'Emlyn, what are you doing up here? Who are you talking to?' His dad examined the bathroom. It was empty, but the walls were covered in moisture from lengthy shower usage. 'What's going on?' he demanded, rounding on his son.

Emlyn cast his eyes for something to save him. Fanny was waggling her fingers oddly, interlocking them and making them wiggle.

'Spider!' Emlyn blurted. 'There was a massive spider. In the tub. I flushed it down the plughole.'

His dad scowled and leant towards the bath again, peering at the empty base. When he turned back, his eyes rolled freakishly – the whites showing as he blinked rapidly. When his irises slipped into their usual central position, he pinned them on Emlyn.

Emlyn was taken aback. 'Dad?'

His dad planted a hand on the sink to steady himself.

'Dad, are you okay?'

'Of course I am, you brat!'

Emlyn's jaw almost unhinged itself in stark bewilderment. He reddened and felt the acid tang of bile in his oesophagus. Never – never ever – had his dad spoken to him like that.

'You're always in the way,' his dad added in a hiss, taking his hand from the sink.

Fanny watched, puzzled, from the bathtub. She looked to Emlyn in support, but he was too confused to notice.

'Get out of here,' his dad barked.

'But –'

'*Leave.*'

Emlyn backed off, ruffled and fighting tears.

Always in the way? he thought, brokenly. *Did he really mean that?*

*   *   *

Judge Jeffreys sneered as he directed the man – the boy's father – from the confined space of the bathroom into the hallway. He could see the maid through the eyes of the man he was inhabiting, and while he was fairly certain she had no way of detecting his presence, he wanted to be well away from her, just in case.

He could just make out the shadow of the young lad running down the stairs – his shoes making a loud thunk thunk thunk on the wood.

Yes, boy, he mocked. *Run, run!*

But it wasn't long before the man began fighting to take back control. An inner force – hot energy – battered against Jeffreys' essence and shunted him back into the icy cold of his ghostly existence.

The boy's father sucked in a breath and touched his forehead. His eyes widened suddenly and he ran for the nearest toilet, where he threw up the contents of his stomach in violent, sour burst.

Twenty-One

In his congested head full of *dad-was-so-mean-and-I-met-a-ghost* thoughts, Emlyn forgot to be worried about school. It was not exactly a pleasant distraction from his bullies, but his discovery of awakened spirit maids, coupled with his ferocious dad, just seemed so much bigger than comprehensive school now. In fact, he hadn't even spared a single thought about the loss of his beloved notebook, until it was presented to him, crumpled and curled, by a hand attached to the brightest ray of loveliness Emlyn had ever seen. At least, that's how the words compiled themselves in his brain when he laid eyes on her.

'You're Emlyn, right?'

Emlyn had just entered the school library in his first break period and was about to take his usual seat nearest the window when his world took another dramatic turn. First, he noticed his notebook. Then he noticed it was in the hands of a girl with a neatly cropped hairstyle; brown and bobbed. Her lashes were long and dark, fluttering around deep brown eyes, and her teeth, as she spoke, had a lucky gap at the front.

'My book!' he exclaimed.

Emlyn reached for it, then looked up at the girl cautiously. Was there a catch? Did she want something in return?

'I saw it happen,' she said, placing it into his awaiting hands without further ado. 'I saw it thrown from the bus. My dad had pulled over to answer his phone. He's always taking business calls, you see, and –' She shrugged. 'Well, I got out and grabbed your book before it got too wrecked. Just as well you wrote your name in there, huh?'

'Thank you so *so* much. You have no idea how happy this makes me!' he enthused, clutching the book to his chest before lowering it in embarrassment. Maybe cuddling the thing was a bit over the top? But still. He felt like dancing.

'It's okay. I had a feeling it would be yours anyway. You seem like the type.'

'Type?'

The girl took a seat opposite him now. She had a rucksack on her shoulder, navy with white stars, which she dropped to the floor. 'To write. Stories. Poems. Stuff like that.'

'Oh.' He blanched. 'Do you think so?'

'Hmm.' She pulled out a book from her bag – a plain burgundy school notebook with 'English

Language' written in blue on the cover 'I'm Willow, by the way.'

'Emlyn.'

She smiled brightly. 'I know. I read your book, remember?'

'You read it?' Emlyn blurted. He didn't know whether to be annoyed or gratified. His writing was always a work-in-progress that he kept close to his heart. He never shared it. Not even when his mam pressured him to show her a page of his 'genius' (as she put it).

'You shouldn't be embarrassed. It's really good stuff. I liked the one about the heron that takes a girl from her window ledge and shows her the world at night.'

Emlyn gingerly fingered the pages of his collection. He couldn't look the girl in the eye; he was royally anxious. 'Thanks.'

Willow took a pen from a baby-blue case and opened her school book to the next available blank page. She dated the corner and then stopped. 'You know, there's a creative writing group here. Meets in the library. Thursday nights. For an hour when school ends. They don't usually let first years in, but I can have a word with my sister, if you want? She's part of it.'

Emlyn perked at this, but then floundered. 'No. No, that's okay.'

Willow looked baffled. 'I thought writers loved

groups like that? Like Tolkien and Lewis in their little club...'

'The Inklings?' Emlyn offered knowingly.

'Hmm. Yeah, that's the one. It's good to share your ideas and get feedback, right?'

'I guess so. But in case you didn't notice, I don't ever click with anyone. I'd just get in the way.'

'Pfft!' she said. 'Don't be ridiculous. We're doing fine so far, aren't we?'

He looked surprised. Who was this girl? 'I'm not being ridiculous. It's true. Have you noticed me hanging out with friends? Ever?'

'I noticed you running head first into me when you left the boy's toilets a couple of weeks back,' she pointed out.

Emlyn vaguely remembered the moment he'd made his escape. The girl in his way. His lack of care.

'Ah. Right. Sorry about that. But that also just proves my point.'

'Proves?'

'That I don't have anyone. Mates, I mean.'

'No. You have people that scare you and books you hide in.'

Emlyn frowned at her. 'How old are you?'

She smirked. 'A lady never tells.'

'But you're not in my year, right?'

'Right. I'm a year above you. Eight. And just to go back to our previous trail of discussion… if you didn't click with anyone… do you honestly think I'd be sat here right now? Inviting you to my sister's writing group? Reminding you of the first time we met, even though it wasn't exactly sweet?' She paused and looked at him curiously through those dark lashes.

Emlyn decided right there and then that she was strange. Strange, but wonderful. He almost told her this, but didn't think it wise. In his silence, she focused on her page, gliding the ballpoint in long, loping letters. Forming words that he peeked at, but achieved no sense from as they were upside down and partly shielded by the pencil case.

'You can do what you came to do,' Willow suggested, without looking up. 'Unless you want me to go?'

'Oh. Um. No. Stay. I was just going to do some research, actually.' He didn't think now was the time to mention it was research on the dead.

When she said nothing more, he slid back from his chair and made his way across the room.

Where do I start? he wondered.

And as he looked back over his shoulder at the brown-haired Willow seated in the light from the window, he couldn't help but smile.

A smile full of promise.

Twenty-Two

He googled many things in a short space of time.

How can I protect myself from ghosts?
Are ghosts good?
How can I help a ghost move on?
Why can I see a ghost that no one else can?

There was far too much to read in one sitting. Oodles and oodles of links to websites, blogs and Facebook pages. Not all of them would load because the school network disallowed most non-educational websites, or anything deemed 'iffy.' But with a few interesting hits, Emlyn shed some coins and paid for printouts; various chunks of information he fancied gliding highlighter pens across.

Willow was still at his table when he returned, just as the bell sounded overhead for the beginning of the next lesson. She didn't seem in any hurry as she slipped her notebook away and Emlyn coyly bundled his own notes into his bag, hoping to mitigate his natural clumsiness with silent praying.

'Did you find what you were looking for?'

'Um. Maybe.'

She shunned the rucksack onto her back. 'If you need help looking for something,

I'm your girl.'

'It isn't school-related,' Emlyn offered ominously. *What are you doing? Shut up!*

'That's okay. Probably means it's more fun.'

He smiled as she walked off and took his time to exit the library, even though his history teacher would scold him for tardiness. He didn't want to step on Willow's toes. He needed to process what had happened. Decide whether anything had happened of any significance, or if he was reading into it too much.

He blushed as he thought of her reading his stories, after rescuing his notebook from the clutches of vehicle wheels and rain-spattered concrete.

Would they talk again?

And what would they talk about?

*   *   *

At lunchtime, Emlyn signed up for the next available library monitor opening. He would be issuing books and stamping them for students when the librarian was busy. A newfound confidence had awakened inside him. A sense of belonging. And the library was at the heart of his security. A place for answers. A place for comfort. And maybe even... a place for friends.

Willow wasn't around during the second break period as he'd hoped she might be, but he didn't let it quash the good vibes shaking about in his belly.

He was even starting to make eye contact with people, without being entirely self-conscious about it – all the while keeping his eyes peeled for a flash of that dark chocolate bob-cut.

Don't they say, if you smile at the world, the world smiles back?

It was time to test that theory.

With all the positive developments in school, however, Emlyn still couldn't wait for the day to end. Because – reality check – there was also a dead woman who needed his help.

Monday was a break day for his parents, which meant he could visit the Skirrid at night and talk to Fanny without risk of guests disturbing the peace.

Since Emlyn's encounter with the ghost, time had gone at a tortoise's pace. In the midst of his chemistry class, he'd slipped his blessedly safe notebook beneath his school work and secretly jotted down notes about

Fanny that he thought worthy of recording. Like the steady, warm light in her centre. The creepy, numbing Grey Place. The use of the bell to summon her. Should no one believe his tale, at least it might make an interesting work of fiction.

Leaving his lesson, Emlyn was chipper. In fact, he hadn't been this chipper since his mam had told him he had been such a good boy, Santa (his dad) was stopping by for a cup of tea before delivering presents worldwide on Christmas Eve. And he had, in a jovial manner, sat on the family sofa with what Emlyn eventually suspected to be a pillow shoved inside 'Santa's' shirt, convincing the party he was an overweight man.

'Someone's a jolly green giant.'

Just like that, his mood darkened.

Carwyn was on a corner, just as Emlyn rounded it – the cold-water splash to Emlyn's warm, sun baked stupor.

The bully wasn't flanked by Lee and Ryan (for a change), but still appeared as daunting as ever; his prominent brow cast shadows over his eyes.

Emlyn pretended he hadn't heard.

'Hey, I'm talking to you,' Carwyn snapped, grabbing Emlyn's rucksack.

In that moment, with teeth gritted, Emlyn swung

around. He felt a zap of fury that fuelled his fists and with a whack, he knocked Carwyn so hard in the mouth, the boy's head flung backwards.

Carwyn stumbled and struck the floor, backside first. He clutched his mouth in astonishment at Emlyn's feet. His lip had split, a crimson trickle of blood smearing against his skin.

Never, in all his thirteen years, had a boy punched Carwyn first. Especially not when he least expected them to.

'Fight!' came a squeal of delight from somewhere in the distance. 'FIGHT!'

For Emlyn, who could hear the blood rushing in his ears, the voices of students around him sounded like they were in a tunnel, far, far away.

Carwyn sprang upwards like a lion provoked, claws extended for the kill. Angry and ready for retaliation, his fists pummelled Emlyn's sides.

Emlyn's fragile ribs exploded with a nasty fire. He barrelled into Carwyn and they locked in an awkward combat, their combined weight dragging each other to the shiny, buffed floors.

Students shuffled backwards, giving them room as they roared their appreciation for the madness at their feet.

Emlyn took a smack to the eye that made his head

ring with lightning shocks. He reached upwards with his hand and forced Carwyn's face away.

'Carwyn, stop it! Get off him!' came a scream.

Emlyn recognised the voice. Willow. She was trying to find a way in, pushing people aside.

And then –

Something big intervened, lifting Carwyn upwards and away like a crane shifting heavy cargo. He was jerked into a wall, his chest heaving, and Emlyn was left to stagger to his feet with the help of Willow, who gripped his hand tightly as she pulled him up.

'My office! Both of you. NOW!' barked the school's art teacher, Mr Gubb, his glass-blue eyes wide with fury.

Carwyn wiped the blood from his lip on the back of his hand. He and Emlyn said nothing as the crowd parted – students handing over rucksacks to their thwarted warriors.

Twenty-Three

'I'm sorry we had to call you in, Mr and Mrs Jenkins. But we have a zero-tolerance policy on fighting in school, as you can imagine.'

The Deputy Headmistress was strikingly straight-postured in her high-backed leather chair, fingers laced together and bent into a steeple shape. Her dark hair was wavy and bouffant, frozen in time and space with a tsunami of hairspray. In her petite, gold-framed spectacles, Emlyn could just about make out the reflection of his slumped, defeated body.

He was sat between two very unhappy parents.

'We've spoken to Carwyn Michaelson, who claimed Emlyn threw the first punch. And it seems Emlyn has admitted to this. Now. I'm not as idle as one might think. I know Mr Michaelson has a history of causing, shall we say, disturbances among students, but nevertheless – he has never struck anyone. At least, not on school grounds.'

Emlyn felt numb. Except for his hand, of course, which was still smarting. After an examination from the school nurse, she was adamant nothing had been broken. Just his spirit.

'I'm in shock, in all honesty,' Emlyn's dad said. He was struggling to process that he was sat in a Deputy's office, at his only son's new comprehensive school – a son now bearing a particularly nasty black eye.

'He's usually so good,' his mam offered. She was twisting her fingers around and around in her lap, pinching at her purple coat sleeve from time to time, and tugging it over her wrist. The overbearing smell of her rose spritz perfume invaded the nostrils of everyone present.

'The boys seem particularly tight-lipped about what this was over,' the Deputy Headmistress persisted. 'I've heard nothing but good feedback from Emlyn's teachers on a quick investigation into the matter. So, I'm guessing there's more to this act of violence than meets the eye. However, both boys are to be placed on report for the next two weeks. Longer, should I receive negative feedback.'

'What's a report?' his mam queried tentatively.

'The boys will keep a record book with them. It has to be signed by every teacher they have classes with. And at every registration. With notes on behaviour. Any lateness – any problems during their monitoring – a meeting will be held again to discuss further handling and, should it be necessary, further punishment.' She looked directly at Emlyn now. 'Any missed classes. Any lateness. Any wrong-doings will result in detention after school on Thursday nights. Is that understood, Emlyn?'

'Yes, Miss,' he replied. Solemn. Broken. Bruised.

'Again, I'm sorry to have called you today, Mr and Mrs Jenkins.' The Deputy Headmistress slid her chair back. She stood and reached over, presenting a hand to Emlyn's parents in turn for them to shake. 'I only wish our first meeting had been in better circumstances.'

'Me too.' Emlyn's dad looked to his wife and then to his son.

His eyes were awash with disappointment.

*   *   *

Emlyn was permitted to leave school early with his parents, a crisp green booklet with the word REPORT printed stark and damning on the front. He felt like a criminal on parole, his face swollen and ribs yelping with aches he'd never before had the misfortune to experience.

The car ride was silent. His dad drove, whilst he and his mam stared out the window at the rolling green hills and winding hedges. It was unnatural – how scenery so friendly and inspiring could be the backdrop to a young boy's suffering. The world was golden. Wonderful. Fresh. But Emlyn felt as if it should be a burning landscape now, with dead trees and charred fields.

The familiar sight of their home had lost its warmth. He worried about feeling out of place in his own bedroom. That not even his bed could protect him from feeling so very ashamed of his actions.

I threw the first punch, he thought.

This scared him.

'Follow me into the kitchen,' his dad instructed tonelessly, as he dropped the car keys onto the coffee table with a clatter.

Emlyn gave his mam a furtive glance, but she was pretending the sofa cushions needed fluffing. Thoroughly.

His dad took a bag of peas from the freezer and handed them over to Emlyn. They were cold and crunchy in his hand.

'Put it on the areas that hurt.'

'I'd need an ice bath to cover everywhere,' Emlyn chanced at light-heartedness.

'You know what you did was wrong, Em,' his dad said, serious. 'I don't need to remind you of that. What hurts the most is that rather than tell me or your mam that someone was upsetting you at school, you just lashed out.'

The peas felt heavy in Emlyn's hands as he pressed them to his left eye socket. The stinging sensation ebbed with the icy touch and his mental grogginess faded instantly.

'I thought you could tell me anything. I thought we were friends – as well as being family.' Dad folded his arms and leant against the kitchen counter. Then unfolded them and gripped the side. 'I know you probably think you've failed us. But if I'm honest, I'm more upset about failing you.'

A pang of sadness.

Emlyn could barely look him in the eye.

'Seeing you cut up like this – it's a parent's worst nightmare. Do you understand me?'

A nod.

A sigh from him.

'Are they helping with the pain?'

'It's better,' Emlyn mumbled.

'You'd best go upstairs for the rest of the evening. We'll call you when dinner is done.'

Emlyn made to leave.

'When the peas melt, bring them down. Switch it for the sweetcorn.' His dad turned and picked up the kettle, heading for the sink.

The conversation had been officially terminated.

On his way upstairs, Emlyn's mam stopped him. Without a word or a noise, she hugged him tight.

It was exactly what he needed at exactly the right moment.

'I recognised that lad as he passed us in to the Deputy's office. Carwyn?' she said, as she let him go. Liquid from the peas had dampened her shoulder. She showed no sign of caring about the wet. 'He came to the inn the other day asking for you, didn't he? With two others?'

'Yes,' Emlyn managed.

'I thought they were your mates from school, Em? Why didn't you say? I could have sent them out. Or had a word with them.'

How could Emlyn tell his mam the boys were there to mock them all? To make their business sound like a big fat joke?

He shrugged. 'All the best heroes fight their battles alone.'

'That's not true. No one should fight anything alone. Especially when there are people who love them and would do anything for them.'

He got the message loud and clear, leaving her at the bottom of the stairs where the carpet was prickled with pea-water droplets.

Twenty-Four

When a spike of pain in his sore face woke him around one in the morning, Emlyn was suddenly alert. There came a rush of lurid imagery: The fight. The sound of Willow behind him, calling it to a halt. The disappointment from the teachers – but worst of all, from his parents. And then he remembered Fanny: the bigger picture. All of this nonsense – the bullying; the friendless primary school days leaking into comprehensive. Did any of it even matter when, in the midst of it all, he could interact with the dead?

You made a promise, he thought, empowered now.

Emlyn crept downstairs on tiptoes. He slid his coat over his pyjamas. He retrieved keys from a wonky pot he'd hand-made from clay when he was six. And he left the house in pursuit of the Skirrid Inn.

The ground outside was moist, the air bitterly cold. The world slept and the sky watched him, curious. The inn itself was deadly quiet, as if the very walls were holding their breath as he entered. Dust motes danced as he flicked on the lights.

Hurriedly, he unlocked Room Three and, in the hush of the house, he perched on the bed.

Like a fish surfacing to taste bread on the top skin of a lake, Fanny's face appeared through the duvet, rising up from the bed below.

'Emlyn!' She was astounded. 'Your face! What happened?' She made as if to reach for the bruises, but then pulled her hands back – abruptly aware of how invasive she was being. And it was not in her nature to behave that way.

'I'm sorry I couldn't get here sooner,' he said, waving off her worry. 'There's been some… developments.'

'Those boys?'

He told her briskly of the events that had led to his battered exterior. She frowned and gasped and sighed.

'That's terrible,' she concluded.

'Yes. But. I do have some good news. I think I've found a way to help you pass on. At least, I have one thing we can try. I printed some notes in school. Did some research. There was so much to get through. And so many different suggestions.' He was speaking fast. Fanny struggled to keep up.

'A blogger –' Emlyn noticed her confusion at this word. 'That's someone who keeps and updates a page of their writing online for people to read. Well, she mentioned planting rosemary outside the building?'

'Oh, Emlyn. That's a rumour that has been spread for centuries. It's said to ward off evil spirits; not necessarily help the dead cross over.'

He looked deflated.

'We could try it still. If you wanted?' she encouraged.

'Oh. No. It's okay. I guess we could try something else.' There were some more dramatic options he'd read about, like bringing in a medium to help talk to her, but he didn't see how he could afford something so extravagant. And also, hadn't there been mediums present before? The Judge was still around, so they can't have been that good at moving spirits into a restful afterlife.

'I just –' Fanny sighed. 'I want to know more about

Emily. I feel it like an anchor at my legs. Is there any possible way? With this blog thing you mentioned?'

'Um. Well. Not specifically blogging. I mean, someone would have had to be entirely obsessed with your family tree to be writing blogs about their research.' His eyes sparkled. 'That's a start, though. Your family tree! Perhaps I can trace some relatives for you? There has to be a way.'

'I'm not entirely sure what you're talking about, but your excitement is uplifting,' she remarked, grinning at him.

'I'll make a start as soon as possible,' he promised, feeling his enthusiasm revived.

'Thank you.'

He blushed as his heart raced.

'My pleasure,' he said.

* * *

Judge Jeffreys listened to the boy and the maid babbling away in Room Three and growled low in his throat. So that meddlesome child was back, sneaking in the dead of night. Speaking of fights and how his parents had been displeased with him. Then moving onto the subject of the maid and her woes. Giving her hope.

Jeffreys thought about possessing the boy – having some fun – but his curiosity had piqued when the child mentioned his research into getting Fanny's spirit to pass safely on.

Was there any weight to this mumbo jumbo he spoke of?

One thing was certain, Jeffreys would have to intervene soon.

He didn't like change. And there had been far too much of it lately.

* * *

Emlyn entered the kitchen tentatively the next morning. He'd returned home as the numbers on his robot clock had flickered to two-thirty and was able to steal some sleep before a new school day was announced by his alarm.

His dad was awake and standing with a coffee in his hand, staring out the window.

Emlyn reached for a cupboard, nervous of being questioned. Had his nightly visit to Fanny gone unnoticed? He tried not to breathe heavy, focusing on keeping his heart rate down.

'We're out of most things,' his dad piped up,

watching him now. 'We were meant to go food shopping last night, but your mam didn't feel up to it.'

Emlyn felt the implication that it was his fault there was no food like a spear to his stomach.

'I'll open up the Skirrid, though. Make you some breakfast before I take you to school. There's bits over there. Go sort yourself out first, though.'

Emlyn didn't know how to take his dad's mood. It was sombre yet peppered with kindness. Wary, he hurried himself to the bathroom, washed carefully around his bruised body with a flannel and soap, then dressed in his uniform.

His belly rumbled involuntarily as he grabbed his rucksack and he noticed his dad outside the window, heading to the inn.

With a clunk and clatter, he found him in the Skirrid's kitchen, plucking slices of bread from crumpled plastic packaging.

'The two end slices,' he chuckled weakly. 'That okay?'

'Sure,' Emlyn smiled back.

He glanced around, not knowing what to do with himself.

'Grab the frying pan. I'll do eggs.'

Emlyn did so.

But as his dad took the handle, his eyes went vacant.

They both froze.

Emlyn wondered what he could be staring at. Was the pan dirty? Was he struck with the memory of something he'd forgotten? Was he unwell?

'Dad?' he prompted.

'What?' he barked, his chin snapping up.

Emlyn took a step back.

He was speechless.

'Making your breakfast like you're nothing but a baby. Isn't it about time you learned how to feed yourself?'

Emlyn felt his tongue turn to rock. He struggled to swallow. 'I can make it. It's no trouble,' he offered eventually. 'It's just you said –'

'Forget what I said. In truth, I'm rather fed up with pretending around you. It's time to man up.'

Emlyn's eyes pricked with tears.

'Look at the state of your face. Fighting. Like a commoner. No son of mine comes home looking like he's been wrestling with pigs and lost.'

Emlyn wanted to cover his ears. He felt so vile and ashamed and so very confused. Hadn't they spoken last night in the kitchen? Hadn't they ended things there? His dad hadn't been half as cruel when he'd suggested the coldness of frozen peas to ease his aches and pains.

'Dad. I really am sorry.'

Perhaps his dad was right. Perhaps he wasn't fit to be his son. Emlyn could do better. He could be a better person. He needed to try harder.

His dad blinked. His eyes whitened strangely. It was frightening. Surreal.

'And the oil,' he said, with a sing-song lilt.

'Huh?' Emlyn croaked. Caught off guard.

'Grab the cooking oil. It's in that cupboard.'

His dad went to the oven and turned on the gas, continuing to prepare breakfast with his usual flair and commitment to the plate.

Emlyn watched, mesmerised. Perplexed. He stood apprehensively, his dad cooking whilst singing a Stereophonics song.

The food he presented Emlyn with went down in tasteless, miserable lumps.

And it stayed heavy inside him for the remainder of the morning.

Twenty-Five

The thieves that danced as one in the form of yellow light gathered with a hum and a zip. Together, they turned into their favoured human-shaped mass – orbs writhing like fat earthworms in a tin bucket. Shimmering and shifting, the mass was slow and laborious, but it was enough for them to walk the Skirrid freely.

The Death Bringer was teasing the human boy. Scaring him. Enveloping the child's father with his darkness to poison everything and everyone. It was ghastly and cruel.

' – *The boy can talk with the maid –*'
' – *She should know what is happening here –*'
' – *Tell her –*'
' – *Tell her it's lies –*'
' – *She can warn the boy –*'
' – *Quick! –*'
' – *Help them –*'

But as they lumbered collectively upwards, through wooden beams and cobwebs, they sensed the Death Bringer at their heels and panicked.

With a roar, Jeffreys swiped his mighty fists through the mass of orb-lights and laughed as they scattered into the stone walls.

They cowered there like the cowards they had become, turning off their light so that they might go unnoticed.

It was safer in the dark.

It was safer to stay away.

*   *   *

Emlyn had gone from 'ignored by most,' to 'eyeballed by everyone' overnight. School was bursting with rapid whispers as he walked to his classes, the bruises on his face evident for all to see.

'….fighting!'

'…Carwyn!'

'…on report!'

'…at that shiner!'

'…a loser!'

'…only been here five minutes!'

He marched on and tried not to focus on the voices around him. They could say what they wanted; he'd stood up for himself and that's what mattered.

He'd be old news soon.

He just wanted the day to end so he could get home

and hide in his room. And if he felt up to it, sneak out to see Fanny.

Carwyn wasn't in school that day. The reason for this was a popular cause for speculation. He'd broken his arm (unlikely, because Emlyn had seen the boy moving it just fine in the office when they were forced to explain themselves). He was in hospital with a bleeding brain (again, Emlyn doubted this. If anyone was going to be in hospital with bleeding innards, it was himself!). He'd moved schools. His parents had decided to home-school. His father had clobbered Carwyn for fighting and now the boy was too scared to leave the house. He'd gone blind in one eye. Yadda yadda yadda.

Children had such wild imaginations.

'He's going to get you. You know that, right?' came a voice from behind him. Emlyn was eating a sandwich on a bench facing the school's rugby field and running track when he was disturbed by two looming shadows. Immediately, he chucked his sandwich down for the nearby crows that had been carefully observing him from the rugby posts.

As he gathered his belongings, Lee and Ryan yelled after him.

'He'll get you, Creepy!'

'He's coming for you!'

Emlyn swallowed his fear and left.

*   *   *

Seeing Willow approach him at his desk in the library was more of a relief than Emlyn could ever describe. He'd never felt so glum and lonely – even reading wasn't able to take his sorrows away. He just kept reading the same sentence over and over again.

It was futile.

But then she appeared, her bob extra glossy beneath the library lights. Her cheeks rosy from being outside in the cold. Her smile genuine and crystal clear.

'Hey. How are you holding up?' She sounded sympathetic. The first person in the school environment to be sympathetic.

'Oh this?' Emlyn said with feigned nonchalance, pointing to his beaten face. 'This is nothing. I've looked like this ninety percent of my life, so it's all good.'

She smiled. 'Well, you're joking. That's a good sign.'

He blew his floppy dark hair from his face. Was it hot all of a sudden? He felt stifled. 'I'm lost,' he confessed sadly. 'I don't want to be here. But things aren't much better at home either –'

'I can imagine.' She pulled her books out, as well as a green apple, which technically was disallowed. There was a strict 'No Food' policy, displayed in bold posters all over the library walls. 'I'm a good listener if you want to talk?'

He slumped forward, arms crossed on the table and put his chin against his sleeve, sighing loudly. 'It's fine. Honestly. Just my dad being weird with me. One minute he's his normal, jolly self... then he's grilling me about things that just seem –' He tapered off.

'Seem?'

'Mean,' he finished.

'Perhaps he's under pressure? Stressed? You never know with parents.'

'Hmm. But still.' He grunted.

Emlyn twisted his head so he could lean his face on his arms and stare out the window at the same time. The sky was heavy with clouds. Grey and white. Crows danced in the heavens with hungry calls. Lunchtime was their favourite part of the day. The schoolchildren dropped morsels that were ripe for the plucking. The birds were always ready.

'Hey, can I ask you something?'

'Fire away.' She looked attentive, leaning closer.

'What do you know about tracking people?'

She laughed a little. Gentle. Light. Pretty. 'Tracking?'

'Yeah. Like. Finding out what happened to someone?'

'Facebook?'

Emlyn chuckled to himself. 'No. No. This person would be long dead.'

'Oh. Right. So, you mean, like, ancestors? Digging in to history? Old records?'

'Yeah!' he enthused. 'Yeah, that would be it.'

She tapped her pen against her notebook thoughtfully. 'There's a website most people use. My mum helped my nanna trace some of her family as far as she could before it got tedious. I mean, the tree was so big, she'd need a page the size of a rugby pitch to fit everyone on, so she begged her to call it a day. But Nanna insisted she was related to some ancient queen of England and wanted to be sure.' She rolled her eyes at this.

'Would you be able to help me find someone? If I give you as much information as I can?'

'I can try. No promises.'

Emlyn took out his own notebook and pen, ready to share what he knew on the local Price family of the 18th Century. Finally, he felt like he was getting somewhere. Finally, things were moving in the right direction.

*   *   *

If it wasn't for the report, Emlyn would have left the school grounds and his lessons for quieter territory later that day. A mossy rock on the mountain. Or a vast empty field with its plants succumbing to the onslaught of cold weather. Either way, he wouldn't be traipsing around getting his teachers to sign a pocket-sized booklet, stating he'd been well behaved. He'd hide away somewhere, so people would stop staring at his bruises and saying things about him that blistered his eardrums with their absurdity.

One thing had given him a smile, however.

Willow had given Emlyn her number at the end of the lunch break. Emlyn had given her his. They were ready to dig into his project together. The Fanny Price Project as he'd named it, though he left out the parts about how he could see and hear her. That would have been far too crazy for any normal person to cope with.

The world just wasn't ready yet.

As ever, it was a relief to see his mam parked up and ready to take him home when the day was through. There was small talk as she drove: 'The weather is gloomy;' 'I'm making toad in the hole for dinner. Lots of gravy;' 'You've got some book shaped packages in the house that I smuggled up to your room. Don't tell your dad though.'

Though he said nothing, Emlyn appreciated her attempt at cheeriness. He had mixed feelings. So much happening all at once. But the thing that bothered him most was being around his dad at home, with those unpredictable mood swings.

Emlyn's nose started to run again. Wet streams were staunched with tissues as he sat cross-legged on his bed that evening, quietly tearing open cardboard packages to check the books within. The soft laminated covers. The perfect pages. The crisp black chapter headings. The subtle numbering. The sweet dedications and acknowledgements. The promise of adventure. He loved everything about them.

If in death, he was asked what he loved most about living, it would be books.

'Are you coming down for dinner?' Emlyn's mam hovered in the doorway.

Emlyn tugged the tissues from his nose in embarrassment and stuffed them in his pocket.

'Oh, I'm really not hungry,' he lied, putting his new books on the case against the bedroom wall. It was so full, he had to slot them in sideways above the books that were already lined in rows.

'Look, Em. I'm not asking you tonight. I'm telling you. You have to come down and eat something with us. I think we need it. Dinner time is family time and I feel like, since school started, I barely see you anymore.' She paused. 'I miss you. And I'm worried about you.'

Emlyn lowered the remaining bundle of books in his arms.

'Please. Come down. For me?' she added.

How could he refuse when she looked so sad and concerned?

Emlyn's dad was already at the table, mixing gravy into a pile of mashed swede. He smiled as Emlyn joined him. Emlyn forced a smile back.

'Here.' His mam plonked a sweating glass of ice water on the coaster in front of his dinner plate. Emlyn wanted to put it on his bruised face, instead of drink it. But he resisted the urge.

'Thanks,' he mumbled, before tucking in.

Dinner passed quietly for the most part. It felt good to have a bellyful of hot food. Emlyn had forgotten what fresh, steaming vegetables tasted like. And toad in the hole was right up there on his 'top five meals' list. He loved it when the gravy-soaked batter went soggy, virtually untouched by the oven's heat. His mam was the opposite. She'd always loved the crunchy edges. And he could sure tell as she munched loudly, like a horse at its hay.

'Did you have any trouble in school today?' his dad

queried, as he made a sausage on the end of his fork dance around in the dregs of his mashed swede.

'No. No trouble.'

'You sure? Because if you're still being bullied we can go back in and talk to your teachers–'

The food in Emlyn's mouth felt unchewable all of a sudden. He thought about Lee and Ryan. Their warning. Carwyn was coming for him. What could he do to stop it? How could he make it go away?

His mam reached over and put a comforting hand on his wrist.

'We can help you,' she said.

He didn't believe them. He wished he could – truly – but it didn't seem feasible.

'I'm fine. It's over now. I promise,' he said.

'When the school days are over and you look back on this, you'll laugh. You'll tell your kids stories. You'll write about it in your books.'

Emlyn swelled with pride on hearing his dad's confidence in his writing. The thought of telling stories – writing his own books – was a special kind of magic and the encouragement he sorely needed. His lips formed a smile around the batter as he chewed again.

'You should also be more focused on making some friends. Not battling enemies,' his dad added.

Emlyn wiped his mouth on a piece of kitchen roll. 'I've made a friend, actually. She's really nice.'

'She?' His mam waggled her eyebrows and chuckled.

Emlyn blushed. 'She's just helping me with a project. A family tree.'

'Is she pretty?'

'Mam!'

'Come on, leave it be,' his dad interrupted. Then with a wink to his son he said, 'Of course she's pretty.'

Emlyn placed his knife and fork on the plate. Full and finished.

He had a friend, yes! Oh, glory be! As a matter of fact, he had two friends.

One was pretty.

One was pretty dead.

Twenty-Six

Late that night, Emlyn's phone vibrated. He had earlier pulled it from his bedside table drawer and hunted down the phone charger that had disappeared beneath the bed, plugging it in to give the device some juice.

The number that flashed up wasn't recorded in his phone yet, but he knew immediately who it would be.

Not having much luck. ☹ *W x*

He lowered the phone to his lap and sighed, thinking about how to respond to this. His mind drew blanks, until the phone vibrated again in his hands.

Are you sure this Fanny woman had a sister called Emily? I can see F on here, but I'm just getting her death certificate. Nothing about her family. W x

Emlyn wrinkled his nose and pursed his lips in disappointment.

It's okay, he replied with a flicker of his fingers on buttons. *Thank you for trying. I knew it was a long shot. E x*

That little X depicting a kiss felt strange to him. Was a boy, who was just a friend – a new friend, for that matter – meant to include one? Texting rules had never been anything he'd brought himself up to date on. He had three numbers saved on his phone. Mam. Dad. The Skirrid Inn. They weren't the kind of numbers you put effort into messaging.

We could probably get more information at the town library. They have a historian. Carolyn. She's great. X

Yeah that might work. Thanks. X

You going to tell me what this is all for? X

Emlyn felt a prickling of his brow.

Homework. X

Funny. I'm one year ahead of you. I don't remember researching dead people. And don't forget, you already told me it wasn't school related. X

Emlyn started to type. Paused. Second guessed himself. Then went with it anyway.

You're right. That IS funny! X

Fine! Keep your secrets. I'm going to bed! See you at school x

His belly fizzled with excitement.

Yeah, see you. X

Despite getting nowhere with the ancestry website, he thought everything else had gone rather well.

*   *   *

He couldn't sneak and see Fanny that night. His dad had been up watching television with a fleece throw over his legs and had fallen asleep on the sofa. It was too much of a risk to sneak downstairs and out the door with his dad so close to the exit, and so Emlyn abandoned the idea entirely.

Instead, he lay flat on his bed, staring at the black ceiling and wondered what else could someone do to find out about a dead person.

His head hurt from churning thoughts over and over and he slept fitfully, waking when his sore face zinged, or because he was dreaming about arguing with Carwyn on a school bus with several clones of the bully snatching at him from all angles. All occurring whilst his dad stood watch, his eyes nothing but a brilliant white.

When the robot alarm clock mercilessly thrust its crackly tune into his nightmares, Emlyn woke with a lightning strike idea.

Just speak to her, he thought, decisively. Wasn't that how the guests at the inn did it?

'Call her name,' he whispered to himself, as he checked his phone for any new messages. There were none. But that was fine. What he needed to say to Willow was best done face to face.

* * *

'Hey!' Emlyn called breathlessly, his rucksack bobbing on his back.

Willow turned in a swish of brown hair. 'Oh, hi there. I was just on my way to the library.'

He beamed at her and reminded himself to stop looking like a Cheshire cat.

They walked side by side, other students nudging their way past with bags of crisps and the rattling and rustling of sweets.

'I really need your help with something,' Emlyn began.

'Wow! You really are taking my offer to help to a whole new dimension, eh?'

Emlyn paled.

'I'm kidding!' She bumped his shoulder with her fist. 'Go on. Talk.'

'No. It's fine,' he muttered, sheepish now.

'Hey, I was joking. I'm all ears.'

He held the library door open and she entered swiftly, leading the way to their favoured table. There were a few books left unattended on its surface, but no one claimed them as Emlyn and Willow stood idly waiting, looking around for their owners. Clearly someone had 'read and run'.

'Okay, you really need to keep an open mind with

this,' Emlyn said. He sucked in a deep breath. 'Is it hot in here?'

'You look nervous. Why are you so nervous?'

He looked at the table, focusing anywhere but her eyes.

As soon as he said what he needed to say, she would run. She would get up and leave. She would laugh in his face and tell Carwyn he was right, Emlyn was creepy.

You could change the subject? Tell her something else. It's not too late.

'The anticipation is really killing me. Just spit it out.'

He released the breath he'd been holding. 'I've seen a ghost at the inn.'

She quirked an eyebrow. 'Well, I would imagine so! You've lived there since... well... you were born, I'm guessing? Your parents run it, right?'

Emlyn was dumbfounded that she knew so much already and that she didn't seem phased.

'Right. Yes! Well. I've never seen anything, until recently.'

'Ooh, was it hanging Judge Jeffreys?' she speculated, her eyes wide with awe.

He was impressed. 'No. Not him. It was the maid. Fanny.'

'Well, that's still pretty amazing. And also, it makes sense now, why you were fishing around looking into her family tree.'

'So, you believe me, then?' he said, trying to tame the incredulous tone in his voice.

'I believe that you believe. Plus, I'm very open-minded.'

'Wow.' He felt a metaphorical weight leaving his tensed-up muscles. 'That's a relief.' His posture loosened and he slipped more comfortably into his chair.

'Did she speak?' Willow asked. 'What did she look like? Were you scared?'

The questions came in rapid fire and Emlyn was happy to answer them all. It was invigorating, to have a person listen intently to his words without judging him or mocking in any way. Willow hung on his every syllable, particularly those he lowered his voice for. She wanted to know the secrets. He wanted to share them with her.

'I want to help Fanny move on and I've got an idea that might work. But I can't do it alone.'

'I'm in,' Willow charged ahead.

'Seriously?'

'This village is boring. I've met someone who lives in a haunted house. It doesn't get much exciting than that. I'll help you with the maid. I want to see how this story ends.'

Emlyn grinned from ear to ear.

He'd never been so thrilled.

Twenty-Seven

'Why are you so jittery, boyo?' asked Emlyn's mam from behind the bar, as she spritzed it with antibacterial spray and wiped vigorously.

'I'm not.' He sat on a bar stool, his phone clutched in his fist. His palms were sweaty. He rubbed them, each in turn, on the jeans he'd switched his school trousers for, the moment he'd got home.

'That's the first time I've seen you with a mobile instead of a book in your hand,' she observed. 'Could it have something to do with that friend?'

'She's coming over,' he admitted, struggling to keep the waver of adrenaline from his voice. 'She wants a quick tour before the guests go up. That's okay, right?'

His mam shrugged. 'It's your inn as much as mine.'

Emlyn barely caught the last of his mam's words before the door opened to reveal a friendly smile. The gap between her two front teeth was prominent in the glow of the Skirrid lighting. Willow had a deep purple bike helmet tucked under one arm, an array of daisy stickers stuck to its gleaming surface.

'Willow!' he blurted. 'Hey!'

Be cool.

Emlyn sensed his mam leaving the bar to join his side.

'So, you're the friend Emlyn spoke of? *Croeso!* It's nice to meet you, young lady.'

Willow boldly offered a hand to shake. Emlyn's mam chuckled and took it.

'Nice to meet you,' Willow agreed.

'I'll get the keys.' His mam winked, but Emlyn presented a clinking mass of metal.

'Sorted.'

'Ah! Go on then. But don't get scared now.' She fluttered her fingertips in Emlyn's face and he waved her away, heading on through to the stairway.

'She's mad,' Emlyn commented over his shoulder.

'Least she has a sense of humour. My mam is all business and boredom. The only time she cracks a smile is when Dad books her a spa day in Cardiff and promises a shopping spree –'

Emlyn's legs had a wobble of nerves about them as he hopped his way keenly upstairs to Room Three.

'Fanny's room,' he announced, with Willow at his back.

When he unlocked the door and shoved it open, he came upon his ghost friend instantly – sat on the bedspread with her eyes pressed against her knee caps, crying. Emlyn immediately forgot he had Willow to guide, crouching before the maid at the foot of the bed.

'What happened?' he soothed, trying to see her face better beneath the mass of ghostly tendrils of hair.

Fanny lifted her head. 'Oh! Emlyn. I hadn't heard you coming. I apologise. I didn't mean for you to see me like this.'

'It's okay. Honestly. You don't have to hide from me.' He sat on the bed to console her, then noticed Willow hovering nearby. She looked awkward, placing her bike helmet on the chest of drawers and crossing her arms over her chest, so they weren't hanging uselessly at her side. To her, it looked as if Emlyn were talking to no one.

'I brought a friend,' he told Fanny.

Fanny glanced at Willow.

'Can you see anything?' Emlyn asked Willow hopefully.

Willow shook her head. No.

'You see that bell next to your helmet?' He pointed. 'Ring it.'

Willow did as she was advised, giving the beautiful little prop a tinkle in the silence of the room.

'Now?' Emlyn wondered.

Willow cast her eyes around every corner.

'Nothing,' she admitted, placing the bell back where she'd taken it.

'You spoke of me?' Fanny cut in. 'She knows?'

'She's going to help us,' Emlyn said.

Fanny wiped her watery eyes with the back of her hands. She had been crying because of Jeffreys. He'd spent the morning harassing her. Pulling on her hair. Grabbing about her waist. Demanding stories. Demanding knowledge of her past. She'd begged to be left, but he stayed for as long as he was interested, then disappeared to his quarters to rest.

'Tell me more about your sister, Emily. The places you went. Special places. The happiest memories you have.'

Fanny was intrigued. The lines in her face softened.

Willow was chewing on her lip curiously. Emlyn would have to relay all the information back to her. She could see nothing. Not a speck. And her ears weren't picking up much besides her and Emlyn's own breathing and rustling.

Emlyn pulled his notebook and pen from the deep front pocket of his hooded jumper.

'I'm going to find out what happened to Emily for you, once and for all.'

*　　*　　*

When the weekend arrived, Emlyn was ready – having secreted away some necessary supplies and packed a bag for his expedition. He'd survived school – just about – with no incidents involving bullies and had managed, on the most part, to keep out from beneath his dad's feet. He didn't want any more arguments if he could help it. And he certainly didn't want to be told he was a failure.

It was a time now for adventure and bravery! Like Frodo bearing the One Ring, Emlyn would see his journey to its end. And he was ecstatic to know he had a friend at his side. Like Frodo's Sam. His trusted companion.

Willow arrived promptly at the inn on Saturday morning, dressed warmly and adorned in a navy hiker's rucksack that bulged with items. She left her bike in Emlyn's garden and clambered into the car, taking the front seat on Emlyn's insistence.

Emlyn's mam was overjoyed to see her son spending time with a friend. Getting out of the house. Making the most of the beauty Wales had to offer. It was her utmost pleasure to drive them and she promised, when they were done, to return for them.

'You have your mobile?'

'Yes,' Emlyn assured her.

The two left the car and waved his mam off.

'Do you think there'll be many others around?' Willow looked up, shielding her eyes against the light of day.

'I guess we'll find out,' Emlyn replied, and set off.

They were at the base of the Skirrid Mountain – or the Holy Mountain, according to some. The ground was damp from rain in the night, but the sky was clear and the air fresh, filling their lungs with a silken coolness.

Willow's cheeks went rosy. Emlyn's ears did too.

The walk would take them a good two hours, if they kept a reasonable pace. Neither said much as they gripped the straps of their rucksacks, following the trail through Pant Skirrid wood with their backs bent and legs pumping.

On their way through the trees, they passed a man walking a three-legged terrier dog with a dirty yellow tennis ball gripped between its teeth. The dog hobbled over to say his hellos in warm heavy breaths and then left in pursuit of his owner, who was leaving the mountain behind him with each steady footfall.

'Do you want one of these?' Willow called ahead.

Emlyn stopped and turned. She offered him a cereal bar, which he took graciously. He had snacks in his rucksack, but he liked that she had thought to bring two cereal bars, so that they might share.

'Thanks,' he smiled, tucking in with an earnest chomp.

He did not stop walking to eat, however. They wanted to get their hike over with so they could fulfil their ultimate goal quickly. Rain was forecast for early afternoon and if they could avoid the downpour, that would be a huge accomplishment in itself.

Emlyn hoped this would work from the bottom of his heart and right down to his aching feet. A swift jaunt through woods and over hilltops wasn't the best healing practice for his beaten and bruised body, but if he had to witness Fanny sobbing her heart out one more time, he'd break with her.

'Almost there, I can see the top.'

'They did this for fun?' Willow said, breathlessly.

'There wasn't much else to do back then, besides cloud gazing.'

'Kids today probably won't even know what cloud gazing is.'

The peak was in sight, though a couple lingered by the pinnacle stone, which stated the mountain's name. They stood and posed for photos in their windbreaker jackets and then sat atop a blanket with Paddington Bear printed on, eating sandwiches and sipping from lazily steaming flasks.

'Just sit and eat until they leave,' Emlyn suggested quietly.

Willow nodded and unrolled their own blanket, nodding a greeting to the man and woman who were smiling in their direction. Emlyn set out the food he'd nabbed from the Skirrid Inn kitchen and Willow did the same. Most of it was tasty junk. A variety of crisps and chocolates. But there were brown-bread rolls of corned beef and pickle and two apples, which Emlyn grinned about as he said, 'Aww? Only two?'

Willow nudged him playfully. 'Shut up, idiot.'

They feasted and admired the landscape. A cold breeze ruffled their clothes.

'It makes you appreciate life, really. Don't you think?' Willow said.

'How?'

'All the greenery. Producing our oxygen. We breathe it in. Us; these tiny little specks on a huge mound of rock. There's so much we don't know. So much we haven't experienced–'

'And it could all be over in a snap,' Emlyn interjected, thinking of Fanny. Thirty-five years old. Feverish in bed. Dead.

'People should be kinder. Better.' Willow sighed.

'Not everyone knows how,' Emlyn said.

'Well. We're all just trying to make the most of life. I just wish there weren't people making that difficult.'

Emlyn thought of Carwyn, Lee and Ryan. They made life difficult.

It was then that the couple near them stood up, making a point of waving goodbye and leaving their grassy perch for the descent to the woods.

'Quickly.' Emlyn brightened.

He grabbed three white pillar candles from the depths of his rucksack. A box of matches. And a jar of dirt. The candles he'd found in the store room of the Skirrid. Sometimes, guests left things behind. Sometimes, his mam kept them in a basket of 'things that might come in handy one day.' Candles were a regular forgotten item and the Skirrid had them in abundance.

Now the dirt; the dirt was unique.

After Willow and Emlyn had sat with Fanny in Room Three, to discuss how they might solve her tragic dilemma, the pair had wandered to the cemetery down the road. Protected by St Michael's Church, a cluster of tombstones stood to attention, weathered and woeful.

Willow had been the first to spot it.

The resting place of Fanny Price.

'Take something to remember me by. A token of

my existence. It might help,' Fanny had said. 'Do you know where I was buried?'

Emlyn had spoken to his mam in a curious conversation about the history of their undead residents that night and she'd matter-of-factly informed him, Fanny was 'down the road' at St Michael's.

So, with Willow standing as look out after school the next night, they'd used a garden trowel to scoop up some soil beneath Fanny's stone and squirrelled it away in preparation for their weekend hike.

'Do you want me to try?' Willow asked, as Emlyn desperately tried to light a candle with a match. They kept spluttering out at the wick, the breeze disturbing their progress.

Willow cupped her hand around one as Emlyn lit it and they watched as it remained flickering with life within the barriers of her curled fingers – but only for several heartbeats.

Emlyn sighed defeatedly.

'Forget the candles.' Willow lay hers in the grass and picked up the jar. 'We've got this. And you can talk to Fanny. That's got to count for something?' She opened the jar and sprinkled dirt into her hand. Emlyn presented his palm for her to tip some onto his. Together, with dirt gliding over warm skin –

cascading onto the blanket beneath their crossed legs – they held hands and closed their eyes.

Emlyn's pulse felt like the drums of the school orchestra in his veins. Pounding. Booming. Sending his body into sweaty anxiety.

He opened his mouth, after numerous deep breaths, and with every last nerve shuddering wildly inside him, he commanded the sky to listen.

Twenty-Eight

'Emily? Emily Price?' Emlyn kept his eyes tightly shut, picturing Fanny in his mind's eye. 'I need to speak with you. It's about your sister, Fanny. Are you there?'

Emlyn felt Willow's hands grip a little tighter. Showing her support.

This was not the first time they had tried a seance. In hopes of avoiding the hike all together, Willow and Emlyn had sat upon the bed in Room Three and nervously attempted to communicate with Emily, with Fanny present. But it was to no avail. And it was Fanny's suggestion to take their call to the Holy Mountain; closer to the heavens with a heartfelt family attachment –

'Emily Price. Sister to Fanny Price. Daughter of Laura. I… I'm reaching out from the same place you used to lay and look at the sky with your sister. Fanny said it was one of her fondest childhood memories. That you would remember it too. That you used to spend hours here watching the sun move across the sky. She's trying to find you! Please. Please, speak to us.'

The wind tickled their ears and fed through their hair mischievously.

The two sat in silence for a while.

Willow cleared her throat.

'Emily,' she began. 'Fanny told Emlyn what happened. About the baby. About your mother's death. She told him she had sent word that she was dying of consumption, but she never got to say her goodbyes. She never heard if you were okay. Please. If you could just let us know –'

'Fanny is trapped,' Emlyn added as Willow petered off. 'She can't leave the Skirrid. Her unfinished business is anchoring her there! She's scared. She's alone. She needs you.'

A tap on his shoulder. Was it real, or was he imagining it?

He listened to the world a while, concerned that someone would approach the mountain top and see them, disturbing the focus. Though, without candles lit, they could be considered a couple, in some sort of joint meditation. Not summoning the dead.

Emlyn started to mutter Emily's name over and over.

Thinking very hard about her.

'Emily Price. Emily Price…'

Willow joined in, whispering with intensity.

Another touch. His face. Like fingers running over his cheek, lightly.

'Are you here?' Emlyn asked, suddenly.

'Emlyn?' Willow said, shaking their attached hands. 'Emlyn, open your eyes.' Emlyn felt an army of butterflies skitter and flap about his insides as standing before him, in a soft, translucent wisp of reality, stood a woman.

In the woman's arms, there was cradled a baby.

'Emily?'

She nodded.

Her hair was lighter in colour than Fanny's. Chestnut. The baby in her rocking arms was reaching out towards her gentle face with chubby wrists and fingers.

'I can see her,' Willow marvelled, so quietly, it barely registered in Emlyn's ears.

'You both called to me,' Emily said. 'It was strange. Like a tugging around my middle. I knew I had to come here. It feels... familiar...' She turned curiously around, scrutinising the land. The view.

'We're here for your sister. Fanny?'

Emily's eyes widened. The baby made a cheery, gurgling noise.

'You've found her?'

'Yes! She's been worrying about you, but she can't leave the Skirrid.'

Emily searched the horizon for the Skirrid.

'I remember this place. This is where we played.'

'That's what she told us. That's why we're here.'

Emily's outline flickered. One moment she was clear – almost as if she were a living being, enjoying the view, solid and touchable – and another moment she'd fade to nonexistence.

She isn't meant to be here, Emlyn thought. She's barely holding on.

'Fanny can't move on,' Emlyn explained hurriedly. 'And she's being tormented by the Judge. Judge Jeffreys.'

'I've been waiting for her. Calling to her,' Emily said, sadly. 'I miss her so much. What use is a restful afterlife without the ones you love?'

'She just needs to know where you went. What happened to you. We think it's her unfinished business. Not knowing. If we can go back to the inn and tell her… she might be able to leave.'

Emily touched the nose of her child.

'I got her letter. Heard she was unwell. But she was adamant she'd be all right. That she'd survive. She was always stronger than me. So sure of herself. So clever and iron-willed.' She got the letter! Emlyn thought, awed. And she didn't try to say goodbye? To write back, or visit? He didn't understand.

Emily's face became morose. 'I had lost my baby in childbirth. The cord was about her neck. And I just couldn't handle the grief of it all. Mam, killed and not knowing by whom or why; Fanny, away to work so she could make money for my daughter's upbringing. And then losing my baby after everything we had been through, alone and without a nursemaid or a midwife to help.' She paused. 'I was given the letter whilst still in my robes from the night I gave birth. Bloodied. The young delivery boy… he asked if I needed help. I told him to leave me. I died two days later.'

Willow let out an involuntary noise that sounded like empathy. She squeezed Emlyn's hand and looked to him, her eyes misty. Emily's sorrowful tone was unbearably brittle. It made the skies cloud over in mourning.

'It's all right, child,' Emily soothed, for she could see Willow was touched by her tale. 'I found my girl in heaven. You see?' She rocked her baby. Cooed to her. 'She is the smiling face I mother every day and hold to my chest with a love so bright, it warms me through to my centre. I'm not sad I died when I did. I am only sad I did not send a letter to my sister, telling her how sorry I was and that I loved her dearly.

Explaining my pain. My misfortune. If I had known Fanny would be trapped waiting for word from me, even in death…' Her word failed her now. Her spirit faded and then returned in muted colours.

'We'll go to her. Right away,' Emlyn said.

Emily managed a smile.

'You are kind. I can sense it. I wish there had been kindness in the hearts of men when I was on this hilltop of my youth.'

'I'll save your sister,' Emlyn promised.

'I'll be here for her,' Emily said. 'Tell her come find me. I want her to meet her niece, Anwen.'

The last they saw of Emily's wavering spirit, was the warmth and hope written on her face, before she drifted into nothingness. Savouring her energy.

Emlyn let go of Willow's hands and in haste, they scurried down the mountain – the picnic blanket neglected in dewy, grassy fronds.

Twenty-Nine

Judge Jeffreys heard the footsteps on the varnished beams of the staircase and knew something was about to happen. The sharp, immediate intensity of the feet reminded him of his gavel against polished wood.

Bang bang bang.

Order!

Order!

He was about to lose this game and there was very little he could do about it. He knew this. Had rolled it over in his mind night after night. Day after long, cold day, in the stone walls of his prison.

But that didn't mean he couldn't play a card of his own.

The thieves didn't call him the Death Bringer for nothing...

* * *

'Fanny!' Emlyn bellowed as he took the steps two at a time – Willow at his heels.

His mam had collected them in the car at the foot of the mountain and brought them home, where they darted off in wild elation, storming past Emlyn's dad, who was wiping tables over from the lunchtime madness. Emlyn had snatched up the keys and left his dad to gawp after him in bewilderment.

'Fanny!' He shoved the door open.

Fanny was already at her feet, her face aglow with expectation.

'You found her?' she breathed, body humming with the anticipation of it.

'We found her!' Emlyn confirmed, bursting with joy and triumph.

'Oh!' The light in Fanny's centre shimmered like ice on a window pane. She ran to Emlyn and took his hands, as if she were alive and could hold him. 'Oh, dear boy, you amaze me!' Her hands glided through his arms and torso, but the sentiment was there. 'And you! You have no idea how grateful I am,' she said, turning to face Willow.

Willow was hovering behind Emlyn, unsure of what was happening. Despite their mountain top triumph, she still couldn't see or hear the spirit of the maid. But politely, she waited. Happy to be there.

'She said thank you,' Emlyn repeated, with a grin.

'You're welcome,' Willow smiled, blushing a little.

Emlyn told Fanny all that her sister Emily had shared with them and his words made the ghost wilt a fraction, knowing now that her little sister had died alone, when she had hoped with blind love that Emily would live on and raise her baby happily.

'I know it's probably a lot to process, but, if it's any consolation, your sister was happy. Wherever she's been all this time… it's been nice.' He hoped his words didn't sting too much. The fact that Fanny had been in the Grey Place all that time, alone. The dark reality of her torture by the Judge. It was horrid, no question. She deserved freedom too.

'She's waiting for you,' Emlyn said. 'On that hill.'

Fanny's eyes were wet, but with tears of utter joy.

'I feel so much lighter,' she admitted, marvelling

as a feeling of warmth ran up her toes, circulating through her once quiet system. 'I think… I think I'm ready to leave here.'

Emlyn nodded. 'Try.'

Fanny swirled in the direction of the window. There was no need for doors. There was no need for stairs. She could just leave any which way or how – if her curse had in fact been lifted.

'I'll never forget what you've done for me,' Fanny said and took her final steps towards the world beyond the Skirrid Inn.

Then –

'What the hell do you think you're doing?'

Willow barged into Emlyn in fright, his knees slamming into the foot of the wooden bed. The pair righted themselves, astounded by the sudden interruption.

'Dad… we're just…' he muddled, surprised.

His dad snarled as Emlyn struggled for a reasonable explanation.

'I don't think that's your father anymore.' Fanny stood in front of them. 'It's him.'

Emlyn felt Willow grip his forearm in confusion.

'Him?' He was fixated on his dad's face and scared to speak directly to Fanny too much, when his dad knew nothing of his ability to communicate with the dead. He didn't want to have to answer more questions and give his dad even more reason to think his son was unstable. Unsound. Crazy.

'You couldn't keep that ugly nose of yours out of trouble, could you?'

'Hey! That's not fair,' Willow intervened, stepping forward valiantly. Emlyn put his hand up as a barrier, stopping her from leaving his side.

His dad laughed. 'You two look a picture. And a ridiculous one at that.'

'It's Jeffreys,' Fanny rushed. 'He's inside him somehow. That's not your dad.'

'Inside him?' Emlyn was incredulous.

'What's going on?' Willow demanded.

'Not the brightest star in the sky, are you?' he mocked.

All this time, Emlyn's mind raved. *All this time! All those horrible things he'd said. They weren't Dad. They were never Dad.* He was glad and disturbed, his emotions all rolling into one hefty lump of panic.

His dad hunched a moment, gripping his stomach as if he were pained.

'He's hurting him!' Emlyn cried, to the maid.

'Oh, I'm about to do more than just that,' Jeffreys sneered, picking himself back up again. 'You don't get to tarnish my afterlife without a consequence. Everyone pays in the end. Everyone.'

'What is he talking about?' Willow wanted answers. She didn't know how to process this. Didn't know what was right and who was wrong. Were they in danger? Should she get help?

'Don't,' Fanny begged. 'Stop this. I'll stay! I'll stay if you promise to leave him be!'

'Dad, fight him!' Emlyn yelled. He bolted forward, but his dad used Emlyn's momentum to shove him in the direction of the wall, where he caught himself just in time with both palms flat. His forehead bumped the cool surface of the stone, making his teeth rattle in his skull.

Willow moved to his aid as Emlyn's dad moved onto the landing with purposeful strides.

'What's he doing?' Willow rasped, afraid. 'What's going on?'

'Hurry!' Fanny urged them, standing flustered and useless behind them.

Emlyn tried to pull his dad's hand to stop him from walking off, but again, his dad's strength overpowered him, slamming him into the floor.

Emlyn's coccyx rang with pain, leaving him breathless and unable to stand as it sent a zinging agony through his pelvis and stomach.

'Stop! What the hell is wrong with you?' Willow attempted to touch the man's shoulder, but he swivelled fast and struck her so hard, she let out a sharp yelp.

'Dad!' Emlyn screamed at him. Angry. Worried for his friend.

His dad – Jeffreys – was hunched, pulling something from the banister.

The rope.

The hangman's noose.

The prop his dad had attached to the wooden beam, with its grooves of violent memory.

Like a wild wolf in the throes of a fight, Emlyn leapt onto his dad's back. Willow saw the rope in the man's hand and forgot her stinging face, begging him to stop. Grabbing at him. Dragging him away from the banister.

And all the while, Jeffreys laughed.

He laughed so hard, the true spirit of the boy's father cowered and quivered inside him. Weak. Pathetic.

'Jeffreys, stop!' Fanny hollered.

'Dad, please!' Emlyn sobbed. Tears were running freely from his eyes.

Jeffreys managed to get the hangman's noose over his head and used a back leg to kick the girl away, followed by a harsh buck that sent Emlyn flying on top of her.

And in that moment of freedom, he vaulted the banister –

To plunge to his death below.

Thirty

To the thieves, the innocent man's feet left the banister in slow motion.

Beneath that winding staircase, with the beam above their heads – just as it had been when their lives had ebbed away to nothing – they watched silently.

The cries of the children were a soundtrack of horror that pierced the Skirrid like the days of old. When their own daughters and sons had stood in the court and heard the definitive verdict.

Death.

Death by hanging.

In that instance, they gathered; their orbs became a swarm of fierce light.

They shuttled upwards – the swiftest they'd ever moved in their afterlife – and barrelled full pelt into the stomach of the innocent man with the rope at his neck.

It sent him backwards.

Just enough to see his feet strike the banister and knock him onto the landing, amidst the children.

Safe from the brutality of a freefall that would surely snap his neck.

And with the force of their light, they threw Judge Jeffreys from the man's body, pinning him to the wall, where he writhed and struggled beneath their power.

There was no time for fear.

Only justice.

*　*　*

Emlyn didn't know how it happened. He saw his dad's feet leaving the banister. But it was as if a great wind had blown him backwards and onto the floor, where he lay with the rope about his neck, his eyes closed.

'Dad,' Emlyn sobbed in relief, taking the noose from his neck and throwing it behind him, out of reach.

His dad didn't move.

'Is he alive?' Emlyn wept.

'He is. He's breathing,' Willow assured him, as she leant close to his mouth, sensing the flutter of a breath against her skin.

Fanny was distracted. She was staring at a place on the wall, where all seemed vacant and still.

'What is it? What?' Emlyn asked, frightened that there was more to come.

'There's light,' Fanny spluttered, taking a step back. 'Lots of light. They're...' She shielded her eyes. 'Oh, my...'

'What?'

'T... tearing at him,' she managed to say. 'Pulling him to pieces.'

One of the lights hovered at Fanny's shoulder. She looked terrified, wincing at the sight of it and afraid of what it could do. But the flickering entity rested gently upon her shoulder and stayed there; warming her as the screams of the Judge echoed in her ears.

Lights filling his mouth. Lights yanking at arms. Lights ripping at hair –

'We need to get an ambulance.'

Willow pulled a phone from her pocket. Thumbed in the number. Waited for the response.

Her voice became distant as Emlyn focused entirely on his dad's face. *How could I have doubted him*? he thought.

'Help is coming,' he promised, his bruised face close enough to hear his dad breathing in quiet wisps. He touched his dad's cheek and wished with all his might to see him smile again. To be silly. Playful. He wanted to help him with chores around the Skirrid and watch *Top Gear* re-runs until late.

'I'll do all the ghost tours from now on, to give you

and mam a break,' Emlyn vowed in a loving whisper. 'I'll do anything you want. Just come back to me.'

His dad's eyes fluttered beneath their lids, as if in answer.

*   *   *

The ambulance had come at an exceptional speed, and with it Emlyn's mam, who joined them on the landing, running her hands through her husband's hair until she was asked by the paramedics to give them space.

His dad had come around in a daze – his mouth fogging a clear mask to help with his breathing – and it was an hour or so, and numerous preliminary examinations later that it was announced he'd just collapsed. A result of low blood sugar, perhaps? Working too hard and forgetting to eat? Essentially, no damage was caused.

Oddly, he couldn't recall why he'd gone upstairs in the first place and looked to Emlyn as if he could fill in the gaps. The Judge. The rope. The fighting. It was a void in his memory.

Emlyn and Willow were sat on Fanny's bed with the door propped open, stiff-lipped and irritable. But with his dad flashing a smile of reassurance from the hallway and giving a kiss to his flustered wife, they knew he was going to be okay. That it was over.

'You should go with him,' Fanny said, with a nod in Emlyn's parent's direction. They were leaving for the main house, escorting the paramedics outside with gracious pats to the back and hearty words of thanks.

'Are you going to be okay?' Emlyn asked her.

Fanny put a hand through the wall. All the way through. No barrier. Nothing stopping her from leaving the Skirrid behind.

'I'm going to be just fine,' she said, with the broadest of smiles.

* * *

She saw the dancing strands of her chestnut hair, dazzling in the fading light of day, before she saw the familiar details of her face.

Alighting the Skirrid Mountain, she almost fell to her knees – weak with happiness.

'Emily,' she choked out, ectoplasm tears washing the milky skin of her cheeks.

Emily swirled, her baby clutched to her chest.

And she threw herself upon her sister in a desperate and loving embrace.

Together they cried. Stroked each other's hair.

Kissed each other's cheeks. Held each other tight whilst the baby stirred between them.

'Oh, I have missed you,' Fanny said, wiping her eyes with the back of her hand.

'I thought I'd lost you,' Emily wept.

'I'm here now.' Fanny touched the baby's cheek. Her little niece. So perfect and forever-small. 'I'm here.'

They composed themselves with sniffling laughter and looked across the land, just as they had when they were young. Still holding hands. Not wanting to let go.

'Mam is waiting for us,' Emily said at last, resonating with the memories of afternoons they'd cloud-gazed, bellies sounding their rumble for nourishment.

'Let's not keep her, then.'

The sisters stood – baby Anwen gurgling pleasantly – and together, they took to the sky, like stars tracing an arc through the dusky heaven above.

Thirty-One

The Judge was gone. Obliterated.

The thieves remained, free to play and dance and talk within the confines of the Skirrid Inn.

Before she had left them, Fanny had told Emlyn all that she had witnessed. How Jeffreys' broken pieces had fallen like dust from a neglected bookshelf. Scattering to the floor – chased by the lights of the men he had condemned to death.

The thieves had whispered in Fanny's ear.

' – *We're brave now –*'

' – *We're strong –*'

' – *Won't hurt you –*'

' – *Can go –*'

' – *We'll watch for you –*'

' – *Safe with us –*'

' – *Be free –*'

They would be no trouble, Fanny had informed her living friends. The thieves were not in the habit of doing much else besides knocking over a few picture frames and tapping on a few surfaces, which gave the paying ghost hunters something to tell their friends about, at least.

In the aftermath of a trialling day, Emlyn couldn't thank Willow enough for all that she had done for him. For believing him. For being at his side. His mam insisted she stay for dinner, though it would have to be at the inn – (she was to take the evening shift, now that her husband was in bed resting after his fall) – but Willow politely insisted she was expected home to eat with her family.

Emlyn fretted all evening. Worrying that Willow would decide to hate him now. That she would never speak with him again after his dad had hit her so brutally across the face. But as he arranged his books in his bedroom to keep himself busy, his mobile vibrated.

Well, that wasn't your average Saturday, was it?!! I think I'll be sleeping with the lights on for a while. Hope you're okay. Your dad too! Xx

Emlyn's stomach somersaulted.

We're okay, he texted. *But more than anything, I hope you're okay too.*

Then he finished with two kisses.

Xx

* * *

It was inevitable.

The cruel, heart-crushing reality of it all.

Monday.

School.

Emlyn gripped the handles of his rucksack as his feet glided over those buffed floors, blessed with the knowledge that Mr Bunce and Mr Canning had bumped cars in the school car park, leading to a public argument and sending a fresh wave of gossip rippling through the adolescent masses.

His corridor fight was nothing but yesterday's news.

No one cared.

Except Carwyn.

'Ladies and gentleman!' The bully stepped away from the wall he'd been leaning against and puffed up his chest, making a gesture like a circus ringmaster to an excitable crowd. 'I give you… Mr Creepy!'

Lee and Ryan snorted. Some of the students bustling around them turned to see what was going down, but most kept their feet moving in the direction of classrooms.

Emlyn took a deep breath.

'I'm coming for you, you know,' Carwyn said, keeping enough of a gap between them that no fists or feet could fly and cause damage. Yet.

Emlyn was still poised for an attack – the hairs on the back of his neck rigidly upright.

'It won't be here,' Carwyn added with malice. 'It'll be somewhere outside school grounds. Where they can't suspend me for keeping freaks like you in their place.'

Suddenly, a shadow moved into Emlyn's field of vision.

A girl with a neat brown bob approached Carwyn – an arm outstretched. There was something in her hand, but Emlyn couldn't make out what. A leaflet? A letter?

Lee and Ryan immediately burst into laughter, slapping hands over their mouths to stifle it, whilst Carwyn's face reddened with a flush of hot blood to his cheeks.

'I'll show everyone,' Willow told him, firmly. 'Say one more thing to Emlyn. One more threat. If you so much as look at him wrong, I'll post this everywhere. Facebook. Twitter. School walls. Boy's changing rooms. Everywhere.' Carwyn went to grab it, but Willow snatched her hand away.

'This isn't my only copy,' she said, coolly.

Carwyn grit his teeth.

He gave Emlyn one last hostile stare and then snapped, 'Fine. Whatever.'

He turned and knocked a heavy fist into Lee's shoulder, shoving him away with his pent-up rage.

'Mate, for real?' Ryan chortled, his laughter high-pitched as he flanked his friends.

'Shut up, will you?' Carwyn barked.

Emlyn stared at the back of him as it disappeared from view.

'What on earth just happened?' he asked, bewildered.

Willow flipped the sheet over.

It was a photograph. There were a cluster of children in the picture – about seven or eight years of age – dressed in sheer black leotards and off-white dancing slippers. A determined looking Carwyn was holding hands with a girl in a pink tutu. They were on their tiptoes, their free hands raised above their heads.

'My sister,' Willow said, pointing to the girl at Carwyn's side. 'Ballet classes. He used to go… before he became pure evil, that is. Too bad. My sister said he was pretty good.'

Emlyn smirked. 'This is brilliant!'

'I've had it in my bag since the fight. Fished it out of my sister's album. She made me promise I wouldn't nick it when I mentioned Carwyn was giving you trouble. But desperate times call for desperate measures.' She shrugged and slipped the photo away for safe keeping.

Emlyn wanted to hug her, but the ringing of the bell was a sore reminder of how late he was for his lesson.

'Will she be angry with you?' he asked, as they walked side by side.

'My sister? No. She won't find out! I'll put it back tonight when she's out. And Carwyn won't say anything. He's too embarrassed.'

They came to a fork in the corridor.

Emlyn made to go left. Willow went right.

They paused, grinning sheepishly.

'I'll see you in the library later? Maybe?' Emlyn said, with his heart battering his ribcage. His dark hair tumbled forward, floppy and messy and in need of a cut.

Willow smiled. 'Of course. I'll help you take notes.'

He frowned. 'Notes?'

'For that book you're going to write,' she said. 'About the ghosts of the Skirrid Inn. And about us –' She twisted on the balls of her feet and walked away with the hint of a skip in her step, luminescent lighting bouncing off her hair.

'About us,' Emlyn repeated in a soft, yet fizzling whisper to himself.

He truly liked the sound of that.

Author's Notes

I wanted this novel to feature a strong, sisterly bond at its core. I'm one of four girls and couldn't survive without their wonderful and colourful presence in my life. So, I made the decision to invent 'Emily' as Fanny's close family, though according to her headstone at St Michael's Church, Fanny was married to a gentleman called Henry Price.

I'd like to thank Dr Ashley Owen for her thorough input into this project. You were right about Emlyn needing a friend and my heart swells knowing he's happy at the end of it all.

Thank you to my office pals: Laura George, Michael George and Richard Moss, for listening to me prattling on about plot direction and how I haven't slept because Willow (my daughter) has been keeping me up all night.

Thank you to my mum, sister Nadine and brother-in-law Russell – who did the babysitting when I needed to focus and keep fighting on.

And thank you to The Skirrid Inn! For letting me ask questions. For giving me numerous tours upstairs and for making a very tasty lasagne! May your ghosts be forever active!

A book is never a lone man's journey.

It's influenced by all and published for all.
So, we should celebrate this victory together.
Thank you, again, for your support.

Karla Brading

Emlyn's Poem in full:

Tree of Words
Mum bit into an apple
And showed the seeds within
'If we plant this seed in soil – The life of a tree begins.'

I thought about the apple
As I lay in bed at night
and wondered what else the earth could give
If I planted a seed just right…

When Mum was drinking coffee
And the street was sleepy still
I dug a hole in the garden,
Wrapped up warm against the chill

I put inside that little hole
A book of pages old
And waited days at the window pane
To see its life unfold

A curling wisp of paper white
Sprang up tall and proud
Its tiny leaves had writing on,
Coaxing forth a crowd

The tree grew strong and mighty
And thick white branches spread
With books that dangled high above
Their pages crisp, unread

I plucked one down from the foliage
The people held their tongues
I read aloud a story,
Enchanting parents, daughters, sons

Then –
The Postman wanted a book to keep
The milkman, paperboy too
Old Mrs Marigold, from over the road
And Mr Cooper, with his wig askew

They all reached out and asked me
For a book they could call their own.
I tugged down books, one by one,
Saw to it they were sown.

'There's magic in these pages
There's love and peace and life.
Plant your books in soil!
Plant them all, this very night!'

The crowd left with their prizes
Books clutched against their chests
They dug holes in their gardens
Buried books and went to rest.

When morning came and chased the night
The people opened their eyes
They shook away their sleepy states,
Put on slippers, crept outside –

The world was full of book trees,
Their branches beautiful, heavy!
The people had their stories
The children had so many!

I twirled amidst white pages,
I danced beneath the books
The world shared all its stories,
People planted those they took

And so the books, they travelled.
Every home had its own tree;
Families cuddled up reading
Words are a gift.
You'll see.

pont

THE VALLEY OF
WHISPERS

KARLA BRADING

Praise for *The Valley of Whispers*

'*The Valley of Whispers* is an exhilarating and spirited read. It captures the energy of being nine years old and that unforgettable sense of the school summer holidays stretching endlessly before you but is also a sensitive handling of a terribly tragic event in our nation's history. The main character, Tomos, is struggling with difficult issues in his family life and is also deeply saddened to learn of the disaster which happened in 1966 in Aberfan, the place to where he and his mam have recently moved. Whispers from the past haunt Tomos' dreams and lead to mystery in his waking life, a mystery which is sure to intrigue junior age readers. I found it a very accessible read which, along with broad appeal, should interest reluctant readers. It is a story with a lot of heart, which puts its arms around you and gives you a big hug. I really enjoyed it.'

Ruth Morgan, author of *Alien Rain*, published by Firefly.

*   *   *   *   *   *

'Adventure, mystery and drama... a gripping read for the middle grade age group. I loved it!' Cathy Cassidy, author of *Broken Heart Club*, published by Puffin.

'Karla Brading combines the fun and freedom of summer in a new village for nine-year-old Tomos with echoes of a past tragedy. She does it with a light touch, creating an endearing story with the real-life backdrop of Aberfan. I particularly like the relationship between Tomos and his mam, and the way he accepts that life can't always stay the same. The back cover says that Karla grew up in Aberfan, and she writes about the place with tremendous warmth. This was a very satisfying read which is perfect for kids at the upper end of junior school.'

Sue Wallman, author of *Lying About Last Summer*, published by Scholastic.

*   *   *   *   *   *

'In this quiet tale of a young boy growing up in a valleys village, Karla Brading weaves a haunting spell to deliver a Welsh ghost story with a twist.'

Katherine Roberts, author of *Song Quest*, published by Chicken House.

*   *   *   *   *   *